T0132461

# Still Not Forgiven

*The 1919 Chicago White/ Black Sox And*
*The "Fixing" Of A World Series*

By Timothy E. Adams

iUniverse, Inc.
New York   Bloomington

# Still Not Forgiven

## The 1919 Chicago White/ Black Sox
## And The "Fixing" Of A World Series

*iUniverse books may be ordered through booksellers or by contacting:*

*iUniverse*
*1663 Liberty Drive*
*Bloomington, IN 47403*
*www.iuniverse.com*
*1-800-Authors (1-800-288-4677)*

*ISBN: 978-1-4401-5770-7 (pbk)*
*ISBN: 978-1-4401-5771-4 (ebk)*

*Printed in the United States of America*

*iUniverse rev. date: 8/04/2009*

THIS WORK IS RESPECTFULLY DEDICATED TO:

JAMES H. ADAMS: Who once had to try to explain to a nine year old boy why anyone would ever lose a baseball game "on purpose."

ELIOT ASINOF: For keeping the story alive until I, too, could write of it.

"The Guys:" Eddie, Lefty, Chick, Freddie, The Swede, Bucky, Hap and Joe: As promised, "I told it the best that I could!"

CONNIE ANDREWS: One of the most talented individuals I know for contributing the cover artwork for this project.

*THANKS EVERYBODY.* The Author.

...AND STILL NOT FORGIVEN...

THE 1919 CHICAGO WHITE SOX AND

THE "FIXING" OF A WORLD SERIES

BY TIMOTHY E ADAMS

# INTRODUCTION

In the early Twenty First Century controlling the outcome or "fixing" of a major professional sporting event has become difficult to impossible. There are many factors that have mitigated against such manipulation. The number of individuals necessary to perform the task is often great. The opportunity for secrecy among all participants is slim. The media is omnipresent to expose meetings between players and "unsavory characters." Perhaps the largest factor against the "throwing" of a sporting event is the cost of such a deception. In order to "buy" athletes the modern day gambler would not only need invest a sum that would approximate the salaries of the player participants but also the "winner's share of the event. This money is often substantial.

The main reason that it is now so difficult to "buy" professional athletes is work related income. Public appearances and especially commercial endorsements garner fees for the prominent athlete with much name recognition that is often many times greater than revenue earned within the sport itself. The amount of money necessary to entice a player to forgo these opportunities would be staggering. Gamblers have amassed fortunes without the need to tamper with the activities of professional (human) athletics. As it was put, so poetically, years ago: "never bet on anything that talks."

In the first few decades of the Twentieth Century this was not the case. Gamblers could and did arrange the outcome of athletic confrontations. The most famous of these was the 1919 World Series and the Chicago "Black Sox."

Charles Comiskey loved baseball. The sport was also the passion of "The Old Roman." This having been said, the club owner had a business to run. "Labor" is always a primary cost of any operation. The White Sox saved money in this area of the enterprise. This thrift would eventually result in expense beyond what any sportsman would ever care to pay. The Black Sox were a labor issue that broke Charlie Comsikey's heart. He was not perfect, but Comiskey deserved better than the ending that baseball dictated to him.

Kennesaw Mountain Landis was a noted judge, hired by baseball to do a job. The task was to eradicate gambling from baseball. "The Judge" believed in beginning his operation with an amputation. Eight Chicago White Sox ballplayers had "sinned beyond redemption." Baseball has had no similar scandal since 1919. Landis did what he was hired to do. Today's multi million dollar baseball business might never have come to pass without "KML."

The players who have become known as "the Black Sox." made a terrible mistake. If these men could have viewed their actions in the perspective of more than a half of century later they would have, no doubt, acted differently. These men had no such opportunity. They have been condemned, "forever." I believe that this penalty is excessive. It is the decision of you, the reader, to determine if you consider the penalty appropriate.

The story deserves telling at least one more time. There is little joy in the saga. I hope the journey is informative and heart-breaking. Thank you for bearing with me in my attempt to present you with the information.


TEA 24 September, 2005

# THE 1919 CHICAGO WHITE/ BLACK SOX AND THE "FIXING" OF A WORLD SERIES

## BY TIMOTHY E. ADAMS

# CHAPTER ONE

The saga of the 1919 Chicago White Sox is the story of men. The events that they created and subsequently became involved in were both of human control and lacking of such guidance. As the result of these actions in the World Series of that year, these men were divided into two groups. These groups consisted of eight White Sox ballplayers on one hand and eventually the "rest of the world" on the other.

These categories were not chosen systematically, as in a school-yard "stickball" game, but rather due to the process of elimination. The more politically incorrect the revelations concerning the activities of the eight men became, the fewer were the friends that they could find. Eventually they stood virtually alone.

The activity surrounding these consorts focused upon the "October Classic" of that year. The blunders committed by the eight men, eventually dubbed by the press "the Chicago Black Sox," were compounded by the efforts of others to distance themselves from the eventual "Black Sox Scandal." The trail headed in a direction down which no one wanted to travel. This path would eventually wind through court, the media and into history.

It is difficult to consider the events that this sporting contest would generate without forming an opinion regarding the activities of the participants. This work is not intended to defend or condemn anyone who acted in and around the circumstances of this particular athletic event. To appoint "heroes" and "villains" at this late date would be counterproductive. All of these men (those engaged in the process were entirely of that gender) were ordinary human beings doing the best that they could with the incidents in which they had become involved. Some who had been friends would no longer be so. A few who had been virtual strangers became "bedfellows." Necessity will force individuals to do things, both positive and negative, that they would never have considered themselves capable of only a few years before. The costs of these events would become greater than anyone struggling through them could have ever imagined when the tale commenced. Many of those involved would take those consequences to their graves. A study of the results of these activities should bring no judgments, certainly no "convictions of guilt"- only sadness.

They called them "Black Sox." The entire Chicago White Sox team would face suspicion based upon an unlikely loss to the Cincinnati Reds in the "Fall Classic," of 1919. Ultimately there were only eight baseball players who conspired with professional gamblers to lose this World Series.

Arnold "Chick" Gandil, Fred McMullin, Charles "Swede" Risberg, George "Buck" Weaver, Joseph Jefferson Jackson, Oscar "Happy" Felsch, Edward Cicotte and Claude "Lefty" Williams were vastly different men. They were united, perhaps, in only two things: the first was a desire for more money than the White Sox were paying them. These salaries must be considered paltry even by the thrifty standards of their era. The bitterness of this insulting pay scale would eventually lead these men to seek vengeance from their "stingy" paymaster. This revenge would play out in a legal "blood bath" before an audience that would soon include most of the literate American public.

The second unifying factor was the infamy that their actions would bring to each of these men. The game would never be the same after this octet left its stage. The beauty of Joe Jackson swinging a baseball bat or that of Eddie Cicotte completely befuddling a hitter with a magical "spitball" would be totally lost in the onslaught that would brand the players as traitors to the game that the United States claimed as its own.

It is unlikely that there was ever a little boy who said "I want to grow up to be just like Joe Jackson" or Eddie Cicotte or Happy Felsch or any of the others. Given the circumstances that ended the careers of "the Black Sox" it is impossible to believe that any youngster would ever care to fill one of these roles. The talent of these simple men has been overwhelmed by the publicity of their misguided efforts over a period of less than one months time. Perhaps this is the greatest tragedy of the entire story.

Individuals numbering as many as eight uniting for a universal goal is in itself unusual. This group of eight was the minority portion of the entire unit. How well a group of at least this many interact with each other and with the additional individuals concerned with that same project often determines the outcome of the entire common venture. The eight were a minority of the active Chicago playing roster. Even within this divided team, the vast majority of participants were "playing to win." The numerous members of the non playing organization must have believed that winning just made good business sense. The Black Sox would become an "unholy alliance" within the much larger structure that was the honorable White Sox organization.

Generally combined activities are of a positive nature; this is why many sporting groups are called "teams." For the most part individual differences are submerged to the need to pursue the general goal. While this is seldom easy, men of character generally understand that they are paid to help assure the prosperity of the entire business.

This need to maintain the common purpose is also the reason that the leader of a sports franchise is so critical to the success of the entire venture. One charismatic individual can lead the rest of the performers to heights greatly above the individual abilities of each. Conversely, such a commander can divide and demoralize the group to the point that nobody is performing to potential. In this case, a magnificent possibility can translate into a mediocre performance. Even those who begin by putting their "heart and soul" into their performance can eventually become mentally fatigued by the hopelessness of their exertion. Doomed by this repeated listless conduct the entire effort is predestined to fail.

The President of the Chicago American League team during

this period should be considered a mastermind within his field. This man had led the club to the greatest heights that professional baseball had to offer. The Chicago White Sox had been the World Champions of baseball in 1917. At this juncture the term "World Champion" was not the usual arrogance of those residing within the borders of the United States. The organized game was simply "unknown" outside of the continental political borders of this country. To win in this country did, in fact, indicate championship of the world. This owner would also eventually oversee a plunge of his business to incredible depths. A long life is often as a roller coaster ride, with many sharp rises followed by deep drops. The man they called "the Old Roman" experienced more than his share.

Charles Albert Comiskey the owner-operator of the Chicago White Sox franchise was brilliant. His contributions to baseball as a player included participation on the World Champion St. Louis Browns of the 1880s. He managed Chris Von DerAble's same team to four consecutive American Association titles in that same decade.[1] His contribution to the game in this area and later as an owner and innovator could never be overestimated. When Ban Johnson conceived the idea of the American League, "Commy" would help found the league, play the game, manage a team, and build a franchise all within that new endeavor. Any one of these undertakings would have been enough to make the one who orchestrated the action into a legend. In spite of all of Comiskey's donations to the evolution of the sport and his unquestioned love of baseball, in the end, the game broke his heart.

The eight men who rebelled against his leadership had their own agenda. The efforts of these ballplayers on their own behalf would later be known as a "conspiracy." This lofty term must

---

[1] Victor Luhrs, *THE GREAT BASEBALL MYSTERY: THE 1919 WORLD SERIES*. A. S. Barnes and Company, South Brunswick, New Jersey. 1966. 21.

have confused these simple men. It is unlikely that any of them could have defined the term. At least one couldn't even spell it. To begin to understand the happenings of the 1919 World Series, one must know where the consorts "came from" and what would motivate them more than the allure of another "World Championship" of baseball.

When considering the activities of the Black Sox, one must not forget that these men were already "winners." Only the most talented baseball players in the United States (which was the entire recruiting pool during this era) could ever advance to the major league level. Not only had the eight "Black Sox" excelled on this platform as players they had participated "well" within the team concept. Each of those later indicted for losing in 1919 had taken honorable part as the White Sox had captured baseball's ultimate championship only two years before. The season in between had been interrupted by World War I and never completed. This made Chicago American League Franchise was the reigning World Champion of the sport and heroes to many longing for the return to a peacetime society and the pleasure of simple sport on a warm summer afternoon.

The simple pleasure of the revived sport of baseball would eventually be lost to many of the people of this country. The 1919 season would eventually be remembered most as the year of "the Fix" and "the Scandal." What had changed so much in this short time span that would lead a few ballplayers to betray such hope?

It is a tribute to the genius of Charles Comiskey that these eight players ever functioned as teammates. Those who were involved in the "fix" of a World Series were the core of a team that many consider among the most talented in the history of the sport. In an era before high speed travel and electronic communication accumulating men with baseball skills to the degree that the 1919 White Sox possessed, was akin to catching "lightening in a bottle." There were members of this team who would eventually have their efforts vindicated by baseball's ultimate achievement, induction into the Hall of Fame in Cooperstown, New York. Some of their teammates could have achieved the same status had they not been banned forever from the game after the 1920 season. The genius of Charles Comiskey and his staff had "caught the lightening." Keeping the contents within in the glass confines would soon prove impossible.

Of "the eight" three had never played a big league game with a team other than the White Sox. "Comiskey's people," Chicago scouts and player development specialists certainly deserve all of the credit for the maturation of: Risberg, Weaver and Felsch. A fourth player, Gandil, had originally been a Chicago player, was dealt away and reacquired. Comiskey would probably be forgiven if, late in his life, he had wished that Chick was left in Cleveland and Shano Collins a quite capable and more importantly an unquestionably honest player had been designated to play first base for the Sox for the 1919 campaign. Chick's reputation as a "bad apple" had only grown in the years intervening his play in Chicago. "The fix" would eventually be Gandil's brainchild. The procedure for "taking a dive" would have been beyond the mental abilities of most ballplayers of this era. The "connections" to set such a process in motion were available to even fewer athletes. The disposition to try to put these two elements together in a "get rich quick" scheme may have been accessible to Chick alone.

Sports teams sometimes overlook the antisocialism of an individual player when a spot need be filled for a possible championship roster. This move is almost always a mistake. It certainly was with Gandil. The first baseman's seven "friends" may have been malcontented but it is doubtful that any of them had either the expertise or the desire to organize a swindle of the extent of the loss of "the Series" to the Reds. If the rest were "kindling" Arnold "Chick" Gandil was definitely the "match."

Fred McMullin played a game for Detroit in 1914 and spent the rest of his career with the Sox. This stability was unusual for a "utility" player in this era. Such men were often shuffled from team to team in an effort to solve a short term personnel problem for a receiving club and to create a roster spot for the team for which they had outlived their value and then moved along again. "Freddie" must have had more value to the White Sox than many other men who desired to fill this role on a major league level would have.

Some of this stability, of course, may well also have been attributed to, in part, the sudden end of his employment.

In current terminology the Black Sox were largely "home grown." Only Eddie Cicotte, Joe Jackson and Lefty Williams had any true experience as to the relationship between any major league club owner other than "the Old Roman" and his ballplayers. While there were other owners who were not always gracious to their employees, kindness from them was not unheard of. Connie Mack, owner of the Athletics seems to have been kind to "Shoeless Joe." The gesture of sending an employee to retrieve Jackson to Philadelphia when the frightened young man had "run home" seems more than just a business gesture. It was Mack, as well, who would offer to provide a reading instructor for Joe. "If we only knew then what we know now…" None of the rest of the franchise owners ever seemed to have generated the animosity that was produced between Comiskey and this segment of his employees.

It is important to note that even those athletes that the White Sox had not progressed through their own system to the major leagues were in a Chicago uniform in 1919 because Charles Comiskey was shrewd enough to acquire them, often at bargain prices. It would be difficult to argue that any transaction used to assemble the American League champions of that year had not been to the advantage of the Chicago White Sox.

There was a portion of this team that was incredibly loyal to Comiskey. Many of these men would remain on the Chicago payroll long after their effectiveness as players had ended. It was "the Old Roman's team" and those who followed his lead were often well cared for. The "one who pays the bills" deserves enormous latitude as to how his money is being spent.

Playing baseball in the first two decades of the Twentieth Century was not the opportunity for "fame and fortune" that it would become in the latter part of that time period. The wealthy and the educated normally found more gentile manners of making a living. A baseball game was something that the rich and influential might stop to observe on a sunny Sunday afternoon. As they exited a ball field the "well to do" might marvel at an excellent performance, as they would of that of a first rate actor or a circus clown. These folks were still glad to be leaving the dirt and sweat behind. "The privileged" would never allow their sons to stoop to such a menial occupation. Eddie Collins with his "Columbia education" [2] was the exception, not the rule of professional athletes. Ballplayers generally pursued the career because it was the only avenue that would allow them to use their athletic talents to make a living. Those of the same environment from which ballplayers often came who did not possess similar physical skills were often doomed to a life of poverty in the "mines," "mills, "or 'growing fields."

The only persons who *ever* became rich in the business of baseball were some of the owners of the various franchises. Several owners such as the Wrigley's in Chicago and Jake Ruppert and Colonel Huston in New York were prosperous before they acquired a baseball franchise. These investors had enough capital for the long term. Generally their baseball investment was profitable. The years that the team's accounting was "in the red" it often could be used as a tax write off, hedging other investments. There is value in a diversified portfolio. Others would use a franchise as a means to become wealthy at the expense of the baseball fan.

---

[2]     "Eddie Collins." http://www/baseballreference.com/c/collid01.stml. 1.
Accessed 12 October, 2005.

In the days before enormous television revenue and millions of dollars in products allied to the game, this undertaking was a much more risky adventure. The keeper of the wealth had to be much more conscious of income and expenses when "every penny counted." Still there was opportunity for riches in baseball for those who could operate a franchise in a judicious manner. Usually in business the opportunity for profit is with those who can invest, not those who "work for wages." Charles Comiskey had seen both aspects of this equation in baseball. From each experience he had learned his lessons well. He spent money to make money. Expenditures of fan convenience would be repaid in increased attendance. Public relations money would be returned in wider exposure for the team. Salary outlay had very little return. There were many great players who would work "cheap." After all, in many cases, it was a matter of "where else could they go?" While the American League was founded as an option to the National circuit, there were still only sixteen teams. Few jobs and many applicants always drive salary requirements down. This must have been a delight to Charles A. Comiskey.

This access to riches was never available to the players! "Revenue" and "sharing" were words that would not be seen together in American sports for many, many years. Media exposure and celebrity status would eventually supersede salary in computing player income. The largest portion of this transformation would occur after all of the Black Sox had died. I would dig ditches (not very well at my age) to keep my family from hunger. In 1919 it is apparent that at least eight baseball players would lose a series of games to accomplish a similar mission. "Moral issues" often fall under the pressure of surviving "day to day."

Individual worth within the workplace was also a notion that would not be immediately seized by the American society. This concept would not be fully realized in baseball for nearly another half a century. Joe Jackson knew that he was the best hitter who ever lived. Eddie Cicotte was aware that he was one of the two or three best pitchers of his time. This knowledge was of little comfort. Each were also cognizant of the fact that if they did not sign the contract offer that the Chicago American League Franchise sent them each winter that beginning with the next spring they would never play organized baseball again. So much for self esteem on the job site.

This team shocked the public as had never happened before. Society had adjusted to the advent of crime. Murder, kidnapping and theft had become almost commonplace. In addition the United States had just endured the first (unfortunately, there would be others), "War to end all wars." The carnage of this event was one that US citizens vowed would never be repeated. Those who held out this hope were wrong. There would be another "World War" all too soon...

To many the actions of the "Black Sox" was worse. Eight men had conspired with gamblers to "fix" a World Series. These players would "throw" games in "The Fall Classic" for money. America's "National Pastime" had been defiled. This was "treason." Feelings need not be justified by logic, they exist of their own configuration. Logic would not overcome the sentiment of this generation of baseball fan. Still, if the Black Sox were "criminals" their "crime" did not rival those of death and destruction.

In truth, Benedict Arnold would not have felt at home with the guys that baseball outlawed. These were the feelings of many fans within the American public. "Feelings" as opposed to "thoughts" require no explanation. Ask a mother of a son lost to war if a baseball game is important. Ask the father of a sailor lost in the sabotage of a ship how much he cares of "next Sunday's game." The feeling was "hatred." This animosity would last until at least October 13, 1975. Perhaps it still lingers, all of these years after "The Swede" Risberg's death should have written the final chapter in the saga of the 1919 World Series.

There was little malice in the hearts of the players. After eight baseball careers were ended, they "fought" to go on playing.

Perhaps each wanted to play Bucky Weaver's "one more year for free." They had made a massive mistake, but still wanted to display their talent. Those who continued to play knew that they still had the skills that had made them famous. It would have been much more merciful if time had overwhelmed the talent. Had this been the case these men could have gradually withdrawn from the spotlight.

This process of withdrawal certainly would not have been painless but could have been counted as "inevitable." The mind would have eventually adjusted to the lack of response from the other body parts. It is often the same for a great pianist, with fingers ruined by arthritis or a fashion model ravaged by age. It becomes so hard to gracefully say "goodbye." It must have been worse for these players; for they "knew" that they could still get the job done.

It appears that all of the vindictiveness that would eventually come forth during this saga would originate with baseball's "power structure" and flow downward "upon the heads" of eight nearly unprotected ballplayers. There was never an opportunity for the accused ballplayers to stand and fight in their own defense. A more liberal sports environment of the latter portion of the century would never have settled for this verdict. A better educated, more sophisticated group of athletes would have answered with more venom. The Black Sox had little of that substance within their structure. They lost because they had no words for reply. It is difficult to believe in a disciplinary process in which the only readily recognizable appeal process is channeled back through those who issued the sentence in the first place.

The baseball establishment, led by Kennesaw Mountain Landis cured the disease by "amputation." A retrospective view wonders if less intrusive surgery might have accomplished the same task. If removal was necessary, why did the process stop at eight? Were the legends of some of the others involved in improprieties to large to tackle? Was the "Black Sox scandal" merely a public relations maneuver designed to protect revenue and regain the trust of the baseball fan?

Even the innocent members of the team would be forever stained by the scandal. The magnificent Collinses (Eddie and Shano) the tenacious Ray Schalk, and the master craftsman Red Faber would gain great fame for their baseball expertise. Still, they were members of "that team. " While some on the roster would be remembered as a brilliant player and all as participants on a very good baseball team, the numbers 1,9,1,9 were always included "in the resume." To the innocent it must have felt as a tragedy. All were often seen as "Chicago Black Sox." The aftermath of the actions of some on their roster would change the game of baseball forever.

There were between eight and a million reasons for the actions of the ballplayers involved in this treachery. Eight reasons because each player had at least one need that caused him to betray the American public and his teammates. All of the reasons may never be known. Life is many things but never as simple as mere money. All of the complexities of the 1919 Chicago White Sox are still not understood. No one, therefore, can imagine all of the reasons for their behavior. One more look at the entire incident should be worth the trouble.

In the years subsequent to the 1919 World Series there have been those in baseball who have attempted to portray "The Fix" as an isolated incident. The fact that a few players had gone bad on one occasion was convenient. Baseball was shamed by the Black Sox Scandal. In order to regain the trust and revenue of the American public and specifically the baseball fan these people had to be convinced that the games were not scripted in the manner of professional wrestling. This public relations ploy worked. The baseball business eventually recovered and is today a multi billion dollar enterprise.

The happenings of the 1919 World Series did not occur in a vacuum. A closer look at the facts would seem to indicate that the early history of "The Great American Game" was alive with the attempts of unscrupulous individuals to control the outcome of individual games. These were efforts of amateurs. No one had previously attempted to manipulate the outcome on anything near the grandiose scale of the 1919 World Series. Baseball, on the other hand, had just been introduced to Chick Gandil and Arnold Rothstein.

Prior to 1919 there had been at least one major betting scandal in major league baseball. This incident involved the Louisville Grays. Jim "Bad to the Bone" Devlin a pitcher for that team was at the center of this maneuver. It seems that pitchers are always needed in these deceptions. Devlin's nickname would dictate that he was perfect for just such a ruse. Jim was setting a precedent.

Each play starts with the ball in the hands of the man in the center of the diamond. The hurler's efforts from that point can affect each play more than anything else the others in the game can do. This is the reason good pitchers are usually paid so well and trusted so highly, especially subsequent to 1919, Eddie Cicotte and Lefty Williams. Two of Devlin's teammate's outfielders George Hall and Al Nichols conspired with Jim and former club member George Bechtel to lose for money.[3] The critical piece of evidence had been a wire from Bechtel to Devlin "I can make $500 if you lose the game today."[4] Apparently, Devlin, Hall and Nichols were "takers."

George Hall was the first player to admit wrongdoing and implicated his coconspirators.[5] It seems as though the "criminal code of silence" did not extend between the white lines for baseball players. This embarrassment did not involve "old, washed up" competitors. Devlin and Hall were each twenty eight at the time of their suspension. Al Nichols was in his third year of major

---

3    "Banished From Baseball" available from http: www.1919blacksox.com/bansihed.htm, 2.
4    Ibid. 1.
5    Ibid. Accessed 10 October, 2005.

league play.

It seems as though there was little drama in a suspension from baseball in the 19th Century. If appeals on behalf of this group were attempted, I have found no record of the proceedings. While none of those implicated had "Hall of Fame credentials" each was eventually added to the "Permanently Ineligible for Induction" list of that group.

The series with Hartford was so badly played that it caused suspicion. It has been recorded that the reason for this player action was the failure of the Kentucky team to pay monthly player salaries[6] "Not being paid" frequently makes employees bitter. Louisville club President Charles Chase had little choice but to investigate. The reputation that Chase was protecting was his own. The league backed his decision. Management was all in the business together. If action had not been instigated immediately some stigma might become attached to the team that chose to use player services without compensating them for their skills.

National League President William Hulbert followed with an independent investigation.[7] When the plot was discovered all of these players were disqualified from further competition. It has not been reported as to when the Louisville team began to disperse paychecks again. The symptom was treated but the disease had not been cured. Through the first two decades of the Twentieth Century baseball ignored betting. Gamblers continued to frequent ballparks and associate with players. When sins go unpunished, there is little need for repentance. It would take even more to send a "wake up call" to baseball.

Harold Homer "Prince Hal" Chase (apparently no relation to Charles) was a fine first baseman of the late "Dead Ball" era. At Six feet one and one hundred seventy five pounds Chase was

---

[6]     Eliot Asinov, *EIGHT MEN OUT* (New York, Henry Holt and Company, 1963). 12.

[7]     Eliot Asinov *EIGHT MEN OUT* (New York, Henry Holt and Company, 1963). 11

considered tall and thin. Hal was an unusual ballplayer in that he threw with his left hand while hitting from the right side of the plate. The one step advantage to a left handed hitter heading to first base is not an edge often surrendered. Chase was also notorious for his association with gamblers. In 1917 while playing with the Cincinnati Reds, Chase attempted to bribe teammate Johnny Ring to lose a game that Chase had wagered upon. The suggestion was made in the middle of the game! When the offer was discovered the National League held a hearing. Somehow, Chase was acquitted. Reds manager Christy Mathewson vowed that Chase would never play for that team again.

Chase has been called "among the most unsavory characters in the history of the game. He was considered by contemporary observers to be the best fielding first baseman ever, but he, repeatedly, through games for the quick money he could make betting against his own team... He led the leagues first basemen in errors seven times...He holds the AL career mark for errors (285)."[8]

Hal Chase was never particularly team oriented in the first place. In 1914 he "jumped" his contract with the Chicago White Sox to sign with Buffalo of the Federal League. At the demise of the newest league, Chase moved on to Cincinnati (and his famous incident with Ring.) Chase played for five different teams in three different leagues during his colorful career. He may have moved so often merely because some believed him "more trouble than he was worth."

Unbelievably after the "Ring incident" Hal was allowed to continue his career with the New York Giants who were apparently not as "picky"[9] as the first sacker's former squad. Giant manager John McGraw always had confidence in his ability "to

---

8    http://www.baseballlibrary.com/baseballlibrary/ballplayers/C/Chase_Hal.stm. Accessed 11 October, 2005.

9    Asinof, *EIGHT MEN OUT.*, 14.

reform the wayward"[10] kept Chase on board through the 1919 season At the conclusion of that year, even McGraw had seen enough. Chase was released and his playing career was over. Hal had enjoyed a nice long career in baseball. He played for years with everyone in whichever league he was performing in knew that he was helping to "rig" baseball games for his gambling friends. Retribution for "Prince Hal" was extremely slow in coming. Eventually however the first sacker may have been the most worthy member of the Hall of Fame's "permanently ineligible for induction" list. Immortality arrives in many different forms

---

[10]    http://www.baseballlibrary.com/baseballibrary/ballplayers/C/Chase_ Hat.stm. Accessed 11 October, 2005.

# CHAPTER TWO

Baseball has been called "the little boys' game. " While the sport was conceived by "grown ups" and played professionally by adults, baseball has the spirit of "a little boy." It is best played on a green pasture on a warm summer day for the innocent. Joe Jackson played baseball in this manner. While the game would take him far from home, he loved it best in the South Carolina fields of his youth. Joe was employed for his phenomenal ability to swing a piece of lumber. Jackson was not indifferent as to the other skills of the game but his favorite part was "the love of hitting." Buck Weaver and Happy Felsch performed for the love of defense, caressing the little white ball into a mitt and knowing almost instinctively what to do with it next. Perhaps Chick Gandil and the Swede Risberg participated for the love of money. Why Hal Chase played is anybody's guess. Perhaps the only thing that Chase and the Black Sox ever had in common is each having a place on the Hall's ineligible list.

Most of all the losers of the 1919 World Series may have been involved in a labor dispute "gone bad." A labor dispute has been defined as "a controversy between employers and employees concerning employment, or concerning the association or representation of those who negotiate terms and conditions of employment."[11] The concept of such a disagreement was still in its infancy in 1919. What might have been later considered a classic labor struggle would be completely overlooked. Labor and management disagreed regarding wages and working conditions. Labor had no legal manner of addressing these grievances. Labor acted horribly. When the job action was discovered, the uneducated members of the labor force had few places to turn. John L. Lewis and his belief of "organization" for all American workers

---

[11]  http://www.legal-feninitions.com/labor-dispute.htm 1. Accessed 22 April 2005

was still just a dream. Samuel Gompers had begun to organize skilled workers into groups to push for collective improvement. The American Federation of Labor was not designed to aid "menial" labor such as mere ballplayers. In short- those who were qualified to help wouldn't and those who wanted to help couldn't.

At the center of the ballplayer's problem was the legendary baseball "Reserve Clause." The simple explanation of this portion of the standard player's contract in 1919 is difficult. To those of us who are not attorneys the affect seemed to be that after a player had signed his initial contract with a team the club could renew these terms perpetually. The player was no longer free to sell his skills elsewhere. If the player did not resign with the ball club holding his contract he could not play at all. No owner in baseball cared to trifle with the sanctity of this document. After all, it was their money that they were saving. Compared to the overall investment of the team owners, ballplayers must have seemed "a dime a dozen."

The result of this lack of competition for the services of each individual player was that the salaries of all of these participants were kept artificially low. Most major league athletes of this era had few other options. The average education and marketable skill level would be well below that of those of a comparable age in other lines of work. The athletes were selling the only available asset that most of them possessed- their bodies. These participants could do little else but play baseball.

The situation of the ballplayers was made worse by the fact that the team could trade or sell the player to another organization and the reserve clause continued in force, following the employee to his next location. A youngster who had signed a contract in Philadelphia at age nineteen and was happy and prosperous there could be traded to Detroit for example. If this player would refuse to report to the Detroit Tigers he could play nowhere else in professional baseball. This servitude was not limited by time, only death. The team was holding all of the control for the remainder of the player's career.

The "Reserve Clause" had already withstood challenge in court. In January of 1915 a rival baseball league "The Federal League" had filed restraint of trade charges in federal court. The lawsuit was heard in the Chicago courtroom of Judge Kenesaw Mountain Landis.[12] The Judge withheld a decision in the case while the entire 1915 season was completed. As business leaders often do when prices become unbearable, the owners compromised. Concessions were made by the major leagues to Federal League owners. The new league eventually folded. The players had made no progress and the Reserve Clause was still in place.

The players of the 1919 White Sox were victim of this system. The team was owned by Charles "The Old Roman" Comiskey. A former player and manager Comiskey had been a magnificent innovator on the ball field. He taught his pitchers to cover first base when that defensive player moved to field a ball, Defensive "shifts" for right or left handed hitters were introduced by this man. Players "backed up" each other on defensive plays. No player on Comiskey's team was permitted to stand and observe the action.[13] Comiskey's brilliance carried over into the business aspects of the game with bitter results. He loved baseball, but also owned a team to make money. In order to understand the events of 1919 one must know something of Charles Comiskey. Where Comiskey "came from," what his goals in life were and the future he envisioned for "his" White Sox would change the direction of baseball forever. At the end of his lifetime "Commy" may not have been universally loved but he was universally known and widely respected. The man had come a long way in a seventy two year life.

---

12    Robert Smith PIONEERS OF BASEBALL. (Robert Smith. Boston, Toronto, 1976) 38,

13    Robert Smith PIONEERS OF BASEBALL (Robert Smith. Boston, Toronto, 1976.) 54.

Comiskey was the child of a Chicago alderman who had represented the Irish of Chicago's west side for years. "Dad's plan" had Charlie applying for apprenticeship as a plumber.[14] Instead of learning a trade, young Charlie learned baseball on the sandlots of Chicago's southwest side. An innovative first baseman, Comiskey's career would take him to St. Louis as both a player and manager for the Browns.

When Ban Johnson began to build the new Western League in 1893 "The Old Roman" purchased the Sioux City franchise and shifted it first to St. Paul, Minnesota and then to Chicago in 1900.[15] In this manner a long and "very interesting" relationship between the two men was formed.

It has been said that the American League was Ban "Johnson's gift to baseball." A former sports editor in Cincinnati, Johnson defined the role of a baseball executive. As President of the Western League a series of "swift, opportunistic moves outflanked the established NL"[16] Ted Williams was born to be a hitter. Ban Johnson was born to be a baseball executive.

It was back in Chicago as a founding father of baseball's American League and the owner and absolute ruler of the city's White Sox that would bring Charles Comiskey his greatest fame. The Chicago American League Franchise would outlast all of the characters of the 1919 World Series. Charles' original "Comiskey Park" would eventually be demolished. Minor league teams would "fold" under financial pressure. Many major league teams would change the base of their operations due to financial pressure. For all of the problems that the White Sox would experience, they would endure. That the team continues to prosper all of these years after the 1919 disaster is a tribute to the foundation laid

---

14  http://www.baseballlibrary.com/baseballlibrary/ballplayers/C/Comiskey_Charlie.stm. 1. Accessed 1 October, 2005.

15  Ibid. page 1. Accessed 1 October, 2005.

16  http://www.baseballlibrary.com/baseballlibrary/ballplayers/J/Johnson_Ban/sstm. Accessed 1 October 2005.

by Charles A. Comiskey Senior. Many are of the opinion that Chuck would have asked for nothing more.

The primary area in which this owner saved expense was salaries. This was a characteristic that surfaced several times as former players advanced into team ownership.[17] The pay allotted by Charles Comiskey was disgraceful. The "Old Roman" has been portrayed as "thrifty, the polite word for 'stingy.'"[18] The Black Sox knew no other way of providing for their families. They signed their 1919 contracts and suffered. There would be no other choice for an additional fifty years.

It was only in 1970 when an intelligent, eloquent and articulate hero named Curt Flood risked and sacrificed the remainder of his career to challenge this rule in civil court that the system would change. In 1969 the St. Louis Cardinals had traded Curt Flood, outfielder Byron Browne, Pitcher Joe Hoerner and catcher Tim McCarver to the Philadelphia Phillies. The Cardinals received infielder Cookie Rojas, pitcher Jerry Johnson and most important hitting star Dick Allen. The Cardinals thought they had made a fine deal. There was only one catch. Flood refused to play in Philadelphia and sued to become a free agent. Flood likened the reserve clause to "being owned." [19] He compared his circumstances to "being a slave 100 years ago." The Phillies would not compromise. After Flood has "sat out" an entire season, Philadelphia decided to get what they could and dealt the center fielder to Washington. The Phillies obtained pitcher Jerry Terpko, outfielder Gene Martin and catcher Greg Goossen for Flood. Certainly Curt could take some satisfaction in the fact that none of these players ever performed in a Phillies uniform. The Senators, in one of the final years of the second version of that franchise, were desperate (and perhaps far sighted enough)

---

[17]   Smith, PIONEERS OF BASEBALL 59.

[18]   Ibid. 59

[19]   "Curt Flood." available from: http://www.baseballlibrary.com/baseballlibrary/ballplayers/F/Flood_Curt.stm. Accessed 11 February, 2006. 1.

to allow Flood to play a final season with a contract "sans" the reserve clause. The rest of baseball must have viewed this as a significant enough challenge that they continued to oppose Flood in court.

The case eventually was appealed to the Supreme Court. The justices upheld the lower court rulings in favor of the owners. By the time a verdict was rendered even a positive decision would have been of little good to Flood. The court decision and the labor compromises that the decision mandated would come only when Flood was too old to continue his career. It is almost certain that the people in charge of the baseball structure knew that this would be the case all along. Although he had gained little financially, Curt Flood had won an important victory. Baseball players were not "slaves" after all.

Two other pioneers in this effort were Dave McNally and Andy Messersmith. In 1975 these heroes took a step that would have been impossible during the "dead ball" era. Each played the season without contracts from their teams, the Montreal Expos and Los Angeles Dodgers, respectively. After the 1975 season these pitchers began litigation to obtain freedom from the teams that "owned" them. Dave McNally had recently been plagued by "arm trouble" and had won only three games for the Expos in 1975. After the conclusion of his "day in court" the left hander would not win again in the major leagues.

Of the three only Messersmith ever realized significant financial gain from the process. Andy "went to court" following impressive consecutive years of twenty and nineteen wins for the Dodgers. An arbitrator ruled this pitcher a "free agent." The right handed hurler and his agent negotiated wisely. He was able to obtain a substantial new contract with a new team. Owner Ted Turner and the Atlanta Braves were apparently less bound by tradition and the mores of National League baseball than many other organizations. Turner wanted to win and was ready to spend whatever it might take to get that task done. In the short term this allowed John Andrew Messersmith to obtain significant monetary incentive as well. Messersmith was probably not worth Turner's investment if only games won and lost are considered. Andy would win only eighteen more big league games. The remainder of his career would total twenty two more losses for three different teams.

Actually, money probably meant little to these labor pioneers. They were fighting for the right to sell their service in somewhat of an "open market." This was a right that workers such as plumbers and electricians had enjoyed for years. Baseball players had been deprived of this opportunity for roughly a half a century. In this sense entrepreneur Ted Turner should also be considered a labor hero. Turner was willing to take a chance, betting against all of his fellow owners, to acquire a quality player for his team. In the process, he helped change the composition of the "baseball world." Some have said that since these decisions the pendulum has swung too far the other way-in favor of the players. Others have contended that it "was about time." Each reader must make this decision for themselves.

A rather sad footnote to this entire affair was the disposition of arbitrator Peter Seitz within the baseball appeals process. In December of 1974 Seitz had declared pitcher Jim "Catfish" Hunter a "free agent" following a contract dispute with the Oakland (formerly Kansas City, originally Philadelphia) As. Apparently "Messersmith/McNally" signaled that the owners had seen enough. John Gaherin, the chairman of their "Player Relations Committee" immediately dismisses Seitz as an arbitrator. So much for justice and fair play.

Observers today both marvel and complain of the rights the baseball players have. The positions have completely reversed. The owners still have the money to pay and now do so excessively. Many fans see salary disputes as spats between "millionaire players and billionaire owners." Much of this can be attributed to endorsements, advertising and "the great god" television. The

American public would pay for the convenience of watching their favorite team from the comfort of their own home. Advertisers would pay the networks magnificent sums to put their product before that public during the interludes of such an event. The owners would demand their "cut" of these proceeds. The trickle down of this money to the individual athletes would become an avalanche. It seemed as though everyone was getting rich. All of this was all too little and over fifty years too late for some of the most talented baseball players the game would ever know.

As baseball resumed after World War I major league team owners had agreed to cut salaries to the maximum extent possible. This practice was primarily born of uncertainty. Owners did not know if the crowds would come back after the conflict. Perhaps the aftertaste of mortal combat would destroy the desire of the public for a "game." To most of those who controlled the teams this was seen as a temporary, protective measure. It was expected that salary expenses would be raised again to the normal level as soon as it was assured that the revenue had also returned. Charles Comiskey, owner of the Chicago White Sox was incredibly loyal to this cost cutting bargain.

It would be safe to say that Comiskey was very careful with the money he allocated to player salaries. To be more precise his ballplayers considered him a ""cheap, stingy tyrant."[20] Labor was a mere commodity to the Old Roman. Although the industry was different, Comiskey's theory of labor could be compared to the view of another captain of industry Andrew Carnagie. Of Carnagie it had been said "Carnagie never wanted to know the profits. He always wanted to know of cost."[21] It also was said of Carnagie and might have been could have been said of Comiskey: "You are always expected to get it ten cents cheaper the next year

---

[20]    Eliot Asinof *EIGHT MEN OUT* (New York: Henry Holt and Company, 1963), 20.

[21]    Brody, David. *LABOR IN CRISIS*. (Chicago: University of Chicago Press, 1987), 13.

or the next month."[22] While these business practices may have been considered brilliant in the era of Carnagie and Comiskey, they certainly did not bring "good news" for the employees of these industry giants. Soon eight "ignorant" ballplayers would receive the "bad news" of this philosophy.

In another money making move the franchise owners had agreed to expand the World Series from the traditional four games of seven format, to a five games of a possible nine extravaganza. This experiment would last only two years 1919 and 1920; the club owners agreed that they need increase their profits. This economic theory did not extend to the players. The players portion of World Series profit would still be based upon receipts for no more than seven games. The athletes would be expected to play two more games "for nothing."

By mid 1919 attendance figures had proven the pessimists wrong. Baseball was more popular than ever, but Comiskey's Sox were the poorest paid team of them all. Joe "Shoeless Joe" Jackson, considered by many the greatest hitter who ever lived, never earned more than six thousand dollars. George "Buck" Weaver garnered the same salary. Eddie Cicotte earned less than six thousand... Arnold "Chick" Gandil and Oscar "Happy" Felsch made $4000.00. Claude "Lefty" Williams and Charles "Swede" Risberg got Three thousand dollars.[23] By these standards it is surprising that utility infielder Fred McMullin was paid at all.

In order to comprehend the arrangement of the outcome of this Series, one must know of the backgrounds of these players. In addition to deceit, this is a story of poverty, greed, human manipulation and betrayal. The "why" of this behavior was closely tied to the individual histories of the participant ballplayers.

Joseph Jefferson Jackson was born in Pickens County South

---

22   Ibid. 14.
23   Asinof, *EIGHT MEN OUT*. 26.

Carolina on July 16, 1889.[24] In the "Carolina Mill Towns" of the late Nineteenth Century few could read or write. Fewer still cared who possessed those skills. Jackson's amazing baseball talent took him far from this soft southern world. In 1908 Jackson's talent took him from Carolina to play baseball in Philadelphia. When Jackson was a young player for the Philadelphia Athletics, team owner Connie Mack offered to hire someone to tutor Joe in these skills. [25] Jackson declined this offer. Such knowledge must have seemed irrelevant to the outfielder. This was a decision that he must have regretted later The man Nelson Algren wrote of as "...the best natural hitter to ever wear spiked shoes..."[26]was, in the end, condemned by the lawyers of the big northern cities that he despised so much.

Jackson played few games in Philadelphia before he was traded to the Cleveland Indians in 1910. It was in this city that Joe's hitting talent became legendary. In 1911 the outfielder hit .408 and *didn't even win the batting championship!* Ty Cobb hit .424. About the time Jackson began to know his way around Cleveland, he was traded again- in 1915 to the White Sox. It would seem unbelievable that such a talent would be moved from city to city three times in less than six years. A player of this magnitude could have been cherished as a cornerstone from which a baseball dynasty could be built. Perhaps this could have happened...someplace other than Chicago. The major league years were a time of constant social adjustment for this quiet southern gentleman. Later, he would not view this period as the happiest of his life.

George "Buck" Weaver is universally considered the best defensive third baseman of his time. He was the only third baseman that Hall of Fame player Ty Cobb refused to bunt against.

---

[24]    Pete Palmer and Gary Gilette *THE ENCYCLOPEDIA OF BASEBALL* (New York, Barnes and Nobel Incorporated, 2004) 325.

[25]    Asinof, *EIGHT MEN OUT, 57.*

[26]    Ibid, 293.

This was some compliment from the man who held the major league record for lifetime stolen bases for sixty years and the record for lifetime hits for slightly longer than that. Statistics would indicate that Weaver had enjoyed one of his finest offensive seasons in 1919. His .296 batting average, seventy five runs batted in and twenty two stolen bases would be fine numbers for an offensive specialist. The third baseman had eleven hits in the 1919 World Series, still Weaver was not offensively oriented, he had earned his fame "with his glove." This man displayed all of his artistry in the Series against the Reds. It would all be for nothing.

At twenty nine years old Buck could have expected many more productive years as a major league player. Saddest of all, everyone agrees that Weaver did not take part in the 1919 "sellout." He would later be banned from the game for having knowledge of the "fix" and not reporting his friends to authority. Weaver considered himself not guilty in the gambling scheme. Bucky adamantly campaigned for forgiveness and reinstatement in baseball until his death in Chicago in 1956. Very seldom in sports has the price of loyalty been this high.

Eddie Cicotte is generally viewed as one of the finest pitchers of his era. In his career he won two hundred nine games. These victories included single season standards of twenty eight and twenty nine wins. The second total was achieved in a season that ended with Comiskey resting Eddie for almost the entire month of September. Comiskey's rationale that he was resting Cicotte for the World Series rang hallow when the pitcher finished that season one win short of a ten thousand dollar bonus. Included in "Knuckles'" accomplishments was a 1.53 earned run average in 1917. In that season the Sox could expect to win a game that Cicotte started by scoring two runs. The team usually did. The right hander was expert at two "trick pitches," the spitball and the knuckleball. On occasion he would also offer a fastball and a curve.

Eddie's true value to the White Sox may be best measured by one incident. Claude Williams had declined Chick Gandil's offer to participate in the 1919 "fix." Gandil advised that Cicotte was already involved. Williams queried in disbelief "Cicotte too?" [27] When Lefty was assured that this was true, he too decided to join. Thoughts of money, loyalty and perhaps bitterness must have passed through Williams' mind. Whatever this young man's motives, his agreement was critical to the plot. "The job" could not have been done without pitching. This being the case Cicotte should count as "two." Eddie was responsible for both his own complicity and to some extent that of Williams.

Perhaps one of the greatest ironies of this story entire was that Cicotte "went in the tank" to pay off the mortgage on his farm. As Happy Felsch did, Cicotte tried his hand at bartending after the conclusion of his White Sox career. That this job did not require an "Ivey League education" may have been the reason that two of eight pursued this "second career." By the end of his life Eddie was a forest ranger and sometimes handyman. The hurler must have either overestimated his ability at growing things or sunk with so many others under the weight of the Great Depression. In his post baseball bartending career, there seems to be no record as to the quality of scotch and soda that he mixed.

Joe Jackson played baseball for the love of hitting. Buck Weaver thrilled at his defensive power and the ability to turn opponent's line drives, grass cutting grounders or perfect bunts into White Sox outs. Eddie Cicotte apparently played to finance a passion for farming. The question remains: Why did Chick Gandil participate at all? He obviously didn't do it for the money. Chick may have made more money in his winter rodeo avocation than at his baseball occupation. It was not for prestige as Comiskey's ego could allow no stars on the White Sox to outshine Charles' own light. Gandil apparently did not love the game as much as

---

[27]    Ibid 17.

many others. After the "big score" of 1919 this ballplayer spent the winter drinking and partying back in California. Prior to the 1920 season Gandil demanded a one thousand dollar raise from his salary of the previous year.[28] When his request was denied, Gandil retired from the sport. The lifetime ban from organized baseball was merely academic to Chick.

Perhaps the big first baseman had spent his career waiting for "one huge score." Obviously, Gandil felt that the World Series was that opportunity. Chick received thirty five thousand dollars for his efforts, or lack thereof. While his money was nearly half of the proceeds of the venture, one must wonder if the money was worth all that it cost the hefty Californian. A former major league player with a little flair for public relations might well have added to his income after the playing days were over with speaking engagements and articles that could have totaled more than Gandil's crooked payoff. Then again, Chick had neither flair for public relations and no time nor patience for long term planning. "1919" must have been the biggest payday of his life. It might well have been that Gandil organized the plan additionally as a bitter man intending to get even with his overly thrifty employer. If this was a motive, it may have been the only success "the fix" achieved. Chick Gandil was ruined as a ballplayer but Charles Comiskey was forced to suffer more than his sins deserved. With Gandil that could have been his intention all along. Who knows?

Felsch, center field, Chicago White Sox. The man was "Happy" until October 1919 and plain "Oscar" thereafter. The athletic talent the man possessed was so outstanding that some of his era called Felsch a better center fielder than Hall of Fame member Tris Speaker.[29] Any youngster who has ever chased after an airborne baseball in the warm summer air can understand the

---

28 "Chick Gandil" available from http//www.1919blacksox.com/gandil. htm., 1.

29 Asinof, *EIGHT MEN OUT*, 180.

joy that Hap experienced in the major leagues. The biggest difference being that when many of us caught up with the object- we
dropped it. Happy Felsch never did. Hap still shares the major
league records for double plays by an outfielder in a season (15)
and outfield assists in a single game (4).[30] The joy of the game
was gone for Happy by the beginning of the 1920 season. By
the conclusion of that same season this man's playing career was
"gone" as well.

In the predominantly right handed world of baseball's "Dead
Ball Era" many who threw with "the other hand" were nicknamed
"Lefty." Claude Williams was no exception. Williams was just
entering his prime when he picked the wrong side in the White/
Black Sox rift. When the left hander was beginning his career in
1911 with Springfield of the Missouri-Arkansas league, Cicotte
and Jackson were already major league stars. Williams made
brief, uneventful stops in Detroit in 1913 and 1914. When he
won thirty three games for Salt Lake City in "the Coast League"
in 1915 he came to the attention of Charles Comiskey who purchased his contract for the White Sox.[31] Williams immediately
became more comfortable in the Cicotte, Jackson group. This
kinship would forever exclude him from friendship with Eddie
Collins, Schalk and the others. In some ways this would make his
later actions merely a matter of course.

In some ways Lefty was the most tragic of our eight men.
After grooming in Detroit for a brief portion of one campaign
and the majority of one other and three seasons with the White
Sox, the pitcher's career blossomed in 1919 with twenty three
wins. The next season Williams amassed twenty two wins. At
twenty seven years of age his career was blossoming. After the
1920 season it was over..."dadadadadadadumpdadump- thud!

---

[30]   http://www/b;aclbetsy.com/soxplayr.htm page 2. Accessed 6 August,
       2005.
[31]   "Obituary." *THE SPORTING NEWS.* November 18, 1959. 18.

This has often happened to pitchers with bad arms, bad attitudes, and this time "bad friends."

Lefty was not originally interested in the deal. Chick had to convince him that Cicotte was already involved. Claude has been said to have exclaimed: "Eddie too?" and this knowledge must have sealed the deal. In a sudden moment of recognition Williams must have understood. It would be his "Black Sox" against not only the Cincinnati Reds but also Collins, Schalk, Kerr, Comiskey and the rest of the Chicago White Sox "establishment." While the concept was nearly impossible to comprehend, Williams knew where his greatest loyalties lie.

"It" couldn't have been done without Lefty and at only twenty seven years of age, he probably had the most to lose of anyone. The quiet southerner hung out with Joe Jackson, also from the south and fellow pitcher Eddie Cicotte. "Just say no," was never a viable option. This group had expanded into the eight men. As with the passengers on the Titanic, they all went down together

Lefty Williams received a fee for setting a World Series record for losses by one hurler in a single Series when he dropped three contests. This standard still stands today. After the "Black Sox scandal" was uncovered those in charge of major league baseball decided that returning to the former seven game format would serve public relations and divert some of the criticism of the disaster of the 1919 debacle. With only four losses available to lose the confrontation, it is likely that Lefty's record for defeats will last "forever."

Williams received ten thousand dollars for his participation. This really wasn't much money to pay for the negative place it earned Claude in the record books. Not much money... until one pauses to consider that this amount more than tripled his regular season salary. Two pitchers were needed to accomplish "the devil's own mission", two pitchers there would be.

That Charles "Swede" Risberg was included with the Black Sox is not surprising. The name of the game for the shortstop was money. Joe Jackson once said "The Swede is a hard guy." In the raucous company of major league baseball during this era earning this distinction was some accomplishment. When his buddy Gandil came forth with a proposal, the mercenary Risberg seemed to have no qualms about accepting. At fifteen thousand dollars this infielder was the second best paid player (after Gandil-the organizer,) in this scheme.

Fred McMullin was included for five thousand dollars as rather an afterthought by Gandil and Risberg. In the movie *EIGHT MEN OUT* Freddie overheard Swede and Chick discussing the Series from his bathroom stall. While it may not have happened quite that way, McMullin was included with his friends in their devious plan. Fred's two pinch hitting appearances in the 1919 World Series were inconsequential.

# CHAPTER THREE

There were eight ballplayers (Gandil, Risberg, Weaver, McMullin, Jackson, Felsch, Williams and Cicotte) that would eventually be banned from the game for their activities in October of 1919. History would link these men together more closely than Mrs. O'Leary and her cow. These men traveled in each other's company for only a brief portion of their lives. It was during these years, however, when the 1919 Chicago White Sox became a part of American sports folklore. A few good attorneys or one outstanding baseball "Players Association" might have changed the future of both these players and major league baseball. It could not be expected that enlightened intervention could have proved the players "blameless." Such representation might have, however, reduced the severity of the penalties that the leaders of the "baseball establishment" would eventually invoke. Guilty the Black Sox may have been, constitutionally deprived they were almost certainly were as well.

Numbers seldom tell an entire story. Over the years salary figures are distorted by both inflation and deflation. It takes economic experts to determine buying power from one generation to the next. Baseball statistics are also subject to interpretation based upon changes in rules and playing conditions. To clarify how underpaid the eight members of the 1919 Chicago White Sox that we are studying were some comparisons must be made. The Cincinnati Reds, the National League representative in the World Series of that season, had a Hall of Fame outfielder Edd Roush. The nickname "Big Edd" might belie the outfielder's physical stature, five foot eleven inches tall and one hundred seventy pounds was not "large" even by 1919 standards. On the field Edd was not just "big" but "enormous" in any plan for Cincinnati success. Two generations before the term "superstar" became in vogue, Roush was one. This observer has never heard a discussion of the outstanding outfielders of the early Twentieth Century in which Roush's name was not included.

The White Sox had an outfielder who most believe would have been in this company if it had not been for the scandal: Joe Jackson. Each team had an outstanding third baseman Heinie Groh of the Reds and Buck Weaver for the Sox. The Reds had acquired a veteran first baseman prior to the 1919 season Jake Daubert. The Sox had a counterpart in Arnold "Chick" Gandil. In 1919 these three Cincinnati players combined for four hundred forty nine hits and a .302 batting average. The comparable White Sox players combined for four hundred seventy eight hits and a .313 batting average. These statistics would seem to merit slightly better salaries for the White Sox players. In fact this was not the case. Gandil, Weaver and Jackson combined for salaries equaling only fifty nine percent of those that Daubert, Groh and Roush drew from the Reds. Such a pay differential held true throughout the entirety of the two rosters. One would need to be a fool not to notice these differences. The Black Sox may have been uneducated but they were not stupid.

The Chicago White Sox had two opponents in the 1919 World Series: the Cincinnati Reds and themselves. Chicago had virtually been two teams for the entire season. The aforementioned group formed one clique. The second faction was headed by second baseman Eddie Collins, pitchers Urban "Red" Faber and Dickie Kerr, outfielder John "Shano" Collins joined by catcher Ray Schalk. This assembly was generally the better educated and more gentile of the players. Each group could boast of the outstanding baseball skills of its members. Eddie Collins, Schalk and Faber would eventually be inducted into the major league baseball Hall of Fame. It has been argued that Jackson, Cicotte and Weaver had careers that would have led them there as well- if not for "the fix."

Owner Charles Comiskey strongly favored the E. Collins, S. Collins, Schalk lead batch. The style of the faction led by the Hall of Fame group was much better suited to the public relations approach that The Old Roman used to "sell" his team to the public. The salaries of the various players reflected this preference.

Eddie Collins was the center of antagonism for the Black Sox portion of the team. Collins would have a twenty year major league career. "Bill James wrote 'Collins sustained a remarkable level of performance for a remarkably long time.'[32] ... He (Eddie Collins Sr.) won no batting titles because he played during the same time as Ty Cobb but did lead the AL in stolen bases four times and in runs scored three consecutive seasons "[33] He had been educated at Columbia University. Eddie's son and namesake was a Yale graduate and a three year second baseman-outfielder for the As. There must have been something in the genes. The "senior" Collins' baseball career would include a couple of years as manager of the Sox after Gleason had retired. In short the gentile Collins was everything that the eight conspirators were not.

There were three major league infield combinations always mentioned as the greatest of this period. Eddie Collins was a member of two of them. The famous "100.000 infield" of the Philadelphia Athletics: first baseman Stuffy McInnis, Collins, shortstop Jack Barry and third baseman Frank "Home Run" Baker in the first two decades of the century may have been the finest.

John McInnis was only beginning his pro career with Connie Mack and the Athletics. His nickname was not a reflection of his social habits. His "handle" came from his days on a Boston playground and the shout of a fan "That's the stuff, kid!" Nicknames of generations past were so colorful, whatever happened to them all? After his playing career, McInnis would coach at Harvard for five years. It is beginning to appear that some of the ballplayers

---

[32]  http://www.baseballlibrary.com.baseballlibrary/ballplayers/C/Collins_
Eddie.stm. 1. Accessed 12 October, 2005.

[33]  Ibid.

had more going for them mentally than we have been given to believe.

Jack Barry seems to have been a reliable if unspectacular shortstop. The "spiking incident" of Barry by Ty Cobb is sometimes cited as the reason that the Tigers and not Philadelphia won the American League pennant that season.[34]

"Home Run" Baker hit a total of ninety six of them during his thirteen year major league career. Frank did lead the American League in that category from 1911-1913 but those totals were eleven, ten and twelve. Baker was a clutch performer. He earned his nickname by hitting game winning home runs on consecutive days off of Hall of Fame pitchers Rube Marquard and Christy Mathewson of the Giants. While these certainly were memorable accomplishments, it leads one to wonder why there was no "Home Run" Aaron or "Hit for the Circuit" Bonds. Apparently it was all a matter of being in the right place at the right time. Perhaps the most lasting tribute to the "hundred grand guys" is that they played together without developing any obvious long term animosity.

Grantland Rice immortalized the Cub combination of third baseman Harry Steinfeldt, "(Joe) Tinker to (Johnny) Evers to (Frank) Chance." The latter three at shortstop, second base and first base were of "the impossible double" fame in the words of Rice poetry. That Tinker and Evers detested each other and didn't speak for at least thirty three years, apparently over who was to ride in the cab to the ballpark,[35] seemed to not damage production at all.

Many consider the Weaver, Risberg, Collins and Gandil in the "same breath" with the other two groups. The Sox bunch certainly appears to be as "hard headed" as the North Side aggre-

34    "Jack Barry." http://www.baseballlibrary.com/baseballlibrary/ballplayers/B/Barry_Jack.stm. 1. Accessed 20 February, 2006.
35    "Joe Tinker." http://www.baseballlibrary.com/baseballlibrary/ballplayers/T/Tinker_Joe.stm. 1. Accessed 20 February, 2006.

gation had been. A major object of contention among the 1919 Chicago White Sox was Collins' salary. Collins had the foresight to have his $13,500.00 per annum which he had negotiated in Philadelphia with the Athletics guaranteed if he were sold or traded from the team.

Collins was apparently a very shrewd businessman. While not in Charlie Comiskey's class, Connie Mack was not known as being overly benevolent either. This salary was so obviously disproportionate to that of any of the "Black Sox" that jealousy was certain to follow. "The eight" were bitter and resentful of Eddie Collins. If any of the White Sox did not envy Eddie Collins, they were probably in the minority among all big league players

First "Cocky" and then "Cracker" were rewarded for their loyalty by Comiskey with the opportunity to manage the White Sox after Kid Gleason was let go. Eddie Collins was at the helm for three years followed immediately by Schalk's two years at the helm. Sorry guys; too little, too late. With much of the talent of Chicago American League franchise gone to suspension, neither could garner a first division finish. Eddie Collins finished his playing career back with the As performing for Connie Mack.

In his youth, with a limited view of the world, this author presumed that Ray Schalk was from Georgia. His moniker was "Cracker," was in not? This was not the case, had it been Ray would have had much more in common with "the eight" than was ever the case.

Schalk was, in fact, born in Harvel, Illinois in 1892. The receiver played all but a portion of one season in Chicago. He succeeded Eddie Collins as manager (a player-manager as was sometimes the case during this period) prior to the 1927 season. On July 4, 1928 Schalk resigned as manager choosing to concentrate on playing. His term brought the Sox a 102-125 record. At the conclusion of the season Ray may have regretted his decision. His value to the Chicago team now diminished by the fact that two salaries now had to be paid for what he had once done for a single check he was given his unconditional release.[36] After a very brief hiatus in New York with the Giants (five games in 1929) Schalk would retire as a player

In addition to being an intense competitor, (the actual reason for his nickname, shortened from "firecracker,") Ray had the advantage of playing in proximity to his friends and family. During the periods of his career when things were not going well, the availability extra support must have been comforting. In any case, the small, always hustling catcher was always a great crowd favorite. Schalk may have been the most outraged by the betrayal of his teammates, but the catcher was the player with the most reasons to take "the fix" personally. Not only were his exceptional efforts given for nothing, his kinfolk were close enough to have watched "the lie" in person, should they have chosen to do so. It must have been incredibly difficult to explain to friends and family why the great players who surrounded him were performing so pathetically.

Even during the period in which Schalk performed he was considered a diminutive backstop. A ballplayer standing only five feet nine inches tall and weighing one hundred sixty five pounds was not usually expected to perform everyday big league duties. Ray's endurance belied his physical stature. He caught one hundred or more games twelve times during his career. Such stamina was nearly unheard of during the period in which Cracker played. At the time of his retirement Schalk held the major league record for games "caught."[37]

It should be noted that Schalk was not an entirely one dimensional player. 1922 was his finest season. Hs "usual" defensive job included leading the leagues' catchers in assists, putouts, chances, fielding while committing only eight errors. With the bat, Cracker showed unusual aptitude, he hit for "the cycle" on

---

36    http://www.thebaseballpage.com/past/pp/schalkray. 1. Accessed 14
      October, 2005
37    Ibid. 1. Accessed 14 October 2005.

June 27. The two eighty one batting average and twelve stolen bases were added to his defensive skills for a stellar campaign. Ray Schalk was third in the balloting for the "Most Valuable Player" of the American League that year behind Hall of Fame inductee George Sisler of the Browns and right handed pitcher Eddie Rommell of the Philadelphia Athletics.[38]

When Cracker was rewarded by Comiskey with a job managing the White Sox as his playing career neared its end few in baseball were startled. This promotion would certainly not have surprised the Black Sox. When Schalk did accept that job, "the eight" would be expected to entertain bitter thoughts that they could never be offered such an opportunity. Time would widen rather than heal the enormous chasm from the 1919 White Sox roster.

If the White Sox did not field an entire roster of educated players, the argument can still be made that Comiskey's men were "smart." John Francis "Shano" Collins was an example. Shano broke in with the White Sox in with Chicago in 1910 as a "disappointment"[39] at first base. That year S. Collins hit only .197. He would get better. In a fifteen year major league career Collins would hit .264, very near the overall average of every batter to perform in a major league game. At the conclusion of the 1920 season Chicago traded Shano Collins and Neimo Leibold (both of their every day leftfielders) to Boston. Shano played for the other Sox (Red) through the conclusion of the 1925 season. As with Cocky and Cracker, Shano had his chance to manage. He also had limited success. Boston won only seventy three games under his leadership. The team lost one hundred and thirty four. Another capable man who struggled in a situation in which he had limited opportunity for success.

---

[38]  "Ray Schalk." http://www.thebaseballpage.com/passt/pp/schalkray/ 1. Accessed 14 October, 2005.

[39]  http://www.baseballlibrary.com/baseballlibrary/ballplayers/C/Collins_ Shano.stm. 1. Accessed 15 October, 2005.

It is interesting to note how often in the early development of baseball lineage was a factor. This can be seen by the several "family connections" in this short era of the game. Eddie Collins Sr. sired Eddie Jr. an outfielder for the As from 1939-41. On the other side of this series was Heinie Groh whose brother Lew "Silver" Groh. Silver had played a couple of games for Connie Mack's Athletics during the 1919 season. Connie Mack begat Earl who played five games for his father's "Athletics" in 1910, 1911 and 1914. Charles A. Comiskey Jr. became President of the White Sox upon the death of his father and led the team until the sale to Bill Veeck in the 1950s. Shano was grandfather to Bob Gallagher a pinch hitter/outfielder for Boston, Houston and the New York Mets from 1972-1975. Such occurrences within a relatively small sampling group might indicate that there is "something in the genes" of baseball families after all. In addition to the inherited physical talent that a youngster might possess, any young man would have a head start to learn the finer nuances of the activity from minds as great as Mack, Collins, and Comiskey in many casual conversations within their own household.

Both Ray Schalk and Eddie Collins spent some of their time in the major leagues playing and managing a team simultaneously. In the early Twentieth Century it was not uncommon for teams to employ "player/managers." Hall of Fame inductee Tris Speaker was predominant in this group. Two of those doing "double duty" for the White Sox were Collins and Schalk. Infielder Frankie Frisch would immortalize this idea with the "Gas House Gang." This was the 1934 World Championship St. Louis Cardinal's team.

The theory behind this dual positioning was simple. It was believed that if the manager could keep the best player on the team happy he would have a head start to keeping a winning combination alive for the entire roster.

By the second half of the last century "player/managers" were all but unknown. The only two of the latter period who come to mind immediately are: Solly Hemus of the St. Louis Cardinals from 1959-1961 and Pete Rose who led the Reds from 1984 to 1989. The reason for this modification was, in two words "Lou Boudreau."

Boudreau would amass a "Hall of Fame" career in professional baseball as a player, player/manager, manager and broadcaster 1938 until his death in 2001. As the shortstop for the 1942 Cleveland Indians, Boudreau was named manager under the "best player" theory. All went well with this arrangement until Bill Veeck purchased the Indians in 1946.[40]

Veeck wanted Boudreau to continue to contribute his amazing performance to the Indians roster but wished to replace him as the team's skipper.[41] At this point, Boudreau played his "hole card." If he could not manage, Boudreau wouldn't play. If he were replaced as a player, Boudreau would force Cleveland to lose the best shortstop in the game. Fortunately for Veeck he would eventually come to an amicable conclusion with Boudreau. "The Good Kid" would still be at the helm of the Indians when they became the 1948 World Champions of baseball.

Boudreau's "gamesmanship" would spell the demise of the "player/manager." It would take an extraordinary situation for individuals of the wealth and egos of franchise owners to put themselves in "the Cleveland situation" again. Now a man either plays for a ball club or manages it. The occasion of the combination of the aforementioned duties is virtually unknown.

It is not uncommon for individuals who do not care for each other to coexist within a workplace. Employment is about performing tasks, not making friends. When the work day ends the employees can all retire to a place where, presumably, they are liked. In the continual interaction of individuals during a baseball season, personal frictions are exasperated. Road trips, hotel

---

[40]   http://www.baseballlibrary.com/baseballlibrary/ballplayers/B/Boudreau_Lou.stm. 1. Accessed 16 October, 2005. 2.

[41]   Ibid.

rooms and playing fields provide little opportunity for separation. Animosity between teammates may have ruined nearly as many ball clubs as lack of talent. This having been said, it could be considered amazing that two of our three great infields were torn by individual dissention. Joe Tinker and Johnny Evers, Cub greats, legend has it, did not speak to each other away from the diamond for *eight years!* Risberg and Gandil were obviously not very close to second baseman Collins either. The three had buried their differences on game day for years, until October, 1919.

# CHAPTER FOUR

Had Red Faber been healthy enough to pitch in the 1919 World Series it is likely that the arrangements to throw the Series would never have been possible. Red would probably have started the games that eventually were given to Lefty Williams. Had this not been the case, manager Gleason would have still had much more latitude with his pitching staff. At the first sign of trouble in each of Lefty's starts Kid Gleason would have replaced Williams with Faber and the Black Sox would no longer have had enough personnel at the most critical positions to keep the Series under control. A rotation of Cicotte, Faber, Williams, Cicotte, Faber, Kerr, Faber, Kerr and perhaps Williams one more time, if the Series had gone nine games under these pitching circumstances, almost certainly would have prevailed. Chicago was playing a Cincinnati team that the Sox seemed able to defeat "at will" in this October event. It appears doubtful that Gandil would have even proposed such a scheme under these conditions. The few observers that believed that controlling baseball games was possible knew that the control of "the man on the mound" was absolutely required to perform such a ruse.

The injury of the honest Faber also contributed significantly to the 1919 World Series disaster. Urban Faber was in the fifth year of what would become a "Hall of Fame" career. While "Red" had amassed only eleven wins in 1919, in his career he would total 254 victories.[42] This is a good, but not startling amount of wins. What made Red Faber's career so remarkable was that he won most of his games for the remnants of a White Sox team that in the aftermath of the 1919 season was usually "terrible." Perhaps the Black Sox would have not been led into temptation

---

[42]   http://www.baseballlibrary.com/baseballlibrary/ballplayers/F/Faber_Red. stm. Accessed 30 July 2005.

and their lives would have been entirely different as well, "…all for the want of a horse shoe nail…"[43]

For the 1919 season William J. "Kid" Gleason was the ringleader of this Chicago circus. Victor Luhrs seems to have described the skipper well. "He was as courageous as they come, honest… and sensitive."[44] Gleason is said to have earned his nickname not only for his small size, he was only five feet seven inches tall but also for his boundless enthusiasm for the game.[45] The Kid had a twenty two year playing career originally as a pitcher. During this more than two decade active ball playing career the "Kid" did what he had to in order to help his ball club. While originally a hurler with the Philadelphia Quakers, Gleason eventually played all four infield positions as well as the outfield. In addition to the Quakers Gleason would play for the Phillies, the Browns, the Orioles, the Giants, the Tigers, the Phillies again and the White Sox. Gleason was considered a "scrapper" who performed enough useful tasks for his team to in order to remain in the big leagues for an unusually lengthy time for one who did not possess superior athletic talents.

Had Gleason been known only as a player, his career would have been noted for accomplishments. He was the second baseman on the pennant winning 1895 Baltimore Orioles. This club was headed by a baseball icon John J. McGraw After the legendary "Mugsy" McGraw migrated to the New York Giants, the Kid followed and captained pennant winning teams there shortly after the turn of the Twentieth Century. Being the captain of a baseball team at the turn of the Twentieth Century was much more of an active job than the largely ceremonial effort it would

---

43   "Horse Shoe Nail," available from www.collingsm.freserve.co.uk/e/38. htm.9 December 2004. Page 1.

44   THE GREAT BASEBALL MYSTERY. Victor Luhrs. A. S. Barnes and Company. South Brunswick, New Jersey. 1966. 23.

45   "William J. "Kid" Gleason. http://www/dvrbs.com/CamdenSports-KidGleason.htm. 1. Accessed 4 October, 2005.

later become. Contrary to his nickname of "Little Napoleon," McGraw did allow his captains considerable latitude as to how the game was conducted on the field. Many successful coaches and managers have found that their tactical genius can be best utilized when combined with the judgment of someone who is in the action on the field. The player can often "sense" or capture important moods and rhythms on the field that would go unnoticed even by the most knowledgeable observer standing only a few feet away. This is one reason why both the "player/manager" and "trusted captain" roles, such as those performed by Gleason and later Pee Wee Reese for many magnificent Brooklyn Dodger teams in the 1940s and 1950s have had their "day in the sun" on so many major league baseball diamonds

Some sources credit "Captain" Gleason for pioneering the intentional walk. This procedure has been used for over a century to bypass a team's best hitter to allow the defense to attempt to retire a lesser batter and end an opposition rally.[46] The Kid was smart and the Kid was tough. McGraw recognized these attributes as he named Gleason to lead his team on the field. Charles Comiskey put these abilities to even better use as he assigned the same man to guide his team on the south side of Chicago. Gleason often placed the names of players with temperament similar to his own on the "line up card" of the White Sox teams that he managed.

Upon retirement as a player after the 1912 season Gleason was a coach for the White Sox through the 1917 campaign. He was out of baseball as World War I shortened the 1918 season. 1919 was his first year as skipper of the Chicago club. Gleason was a lifetime "baseball man." He must have expected that leading Comiskey's enormously talented aggregation would be a pleasure. He was no doubt, disappointed in this belief.

---

[46]   William J. "Kid" Gleason. www.baseballlegends.com. Accessed 5 October 2005. 1.

In the 1919 World Series the Reds were also led by a more than qualified skipper. In an "untainted" World Series this portion of the proceedings would probably have been "a draw." Pat Moran had led the Philadelphia Phillies to a National League pennant in his first year as a manager in 1915. After three less successful seasons Moran was relieved of his duties in Philadelphia. Prior to World War One Cincinnati had been managed by Christy Mathewson. The "Big Six" knew something of playing big league baseball. The Hall of Fame pitcher had played for the New York Giants from 1900 to 1916. He had finished the 1916 season hurling for the Reds. During that seventeen year period he had amassed an incredible three hundred and seventy three wins.

As he concluded his career as an active player Mathewson had done a creditable job in the Reds' dugout. Cincinnati compiled a 164-176 record under Mathewson's leadership from 1916 until early 1918.

Life and patriotism can sometimes deal a "strange hand" in an otherwise serene work career. As the 1918 baseball season was suspended, Mathewson chose to serve his country. This heroism was compounded by the fact that the pitcher/manager/soldier was nearing thirty eight years old as he was dispatched to the military campaign. Christy had volunteered for service in the War and was sent to serve in Europe. During the intensity of this life threatening altercation, keeping in touch with his baseball employer must have been far from the mind of "the Big Six." It should also be noted that communications between the battlefield and the American Midwest were tenuous at best during this period of history. Somehow, Mathewson and the Cincinnati ball club fell "out of touch" during his deployment. When he had not returned home in time for the 1919 season, regrettably owner August "Gerry" Herrmann of the Reds had to make other arrangements. Christy's misfortune resulted in Pat's gain; the desperate Reds had to have a leader in uniform. Cincinnati turned to Moran to guide the activities of the team on the field.

It should be noted that in contrast to Charles Comiskey, Herrman was described as "a distinguished gastronome with a special zest for beer of every shade and wurst of every variety."[47] Gerry may well have been a great deal more fun to play for as well. An additional compliment to Hermann was that Mathewson continued in the employment of the Reds until his death in 1925

The saddest part of this story is that the former hurler and manager Mathewson would never recover from ill health attributed to his military service. He would die on October 7, 1925 in Saranac Lake, New York at only forty five years old.[48]

Pat Moran would also fall victim to fragile health. Pat would remain as the Cincinnati manager until spring training, 1924. In March of that year while leading preparations for the season in Orlando, Florida, Moran became ill. As the exhibition season was beginning it was discovered that Pat had contracted "Bright's Disease" The medicine of this era could do little. Pat would manage Cincinnati no more. Moran's condition deteriorated rapidly. His death predated that of his predecessor by more than a year. Pat Moran died March 7, 1924. Moran was forty eight at the time of his death, also much too young.

In the years since the passing of Pat Moran, modern medicine has made remarkable advances. Dr. Benjamin F. Miller indicated as long ago as 1956 that "Bright's Disease" had been a catch all for many kidney diseases.[49]This term is no longer used. It has been determined that the symptoms of "Bright's Disease" are caused by several different kidney difficulties. These afflictions have been divided and in many cases while there has been no

47    Victor Luhrs, *THE GREAT BASEBALL MYSTERY: THE 1919 WORLD SERIES.* A. S. Barnes and Company: South Brunswick, New Jersey. 1966. 25.
48    Gary Gillette and Peter Palmer. "Mathewson, Christy." <u>*THE 2004 EDITION OF THE BASEBALL ENCYCLOPEDIA.*</u> Barnes and Nobel. New York. 2004.
49    "Diseases of the Kidney." Benjamin F. Miller MD. <u>THE COMPLETE MEDICAL GUIDE.</u> Simon and Schuster. New York. 1978. 422.

conquest of the ailment the lifespan of those afflicted have been greatly increased.[50] It was all too late for Pat but, fortunately, in time for millions more.

As a manager he had won two pennants. One World Series and seven hundred forty eight games. His .561 winning percentage as a manager was very good. One can only pause in sadness to think of what might have been...

The rest of the Chicago White Sox players: outfielders Eddie Murphy, Harry "Neimo" Liebold, catchers Byrd Lynn and Joe Jenkins, infielder Harvey McClellan and Pitchers Bill James, Harry Lowdermilk, Dave Danforth, Tom McGuire, Erskine Mayer, Joe Benz and Roy Wilkinson must have spent the season wondering why all of their other teammates detested each other so.

Resentment and poverty had blended eight ballplayers into the fuel for a fire. A "match" would be necessary to ignite the blaze. When rumors began to spread that some members of this Chicago team could be bought, there was plenty of spark around in the form of gamblers. While there were, no doubt, many such entrepreneurs who would have loved to benefit from such a scheme relatively few had the funds needed to finance it. The President of the United States earned a yearly salary of $75,000.00 in 1919. While some gamblers no doubt made more money than this on a yearly basis this sum could be considered a fortune.

The eight players had decided upon $80,000 as their fee for complicity. While the exact formula for this amount was unclear, this fee was substantial. Cicotte had insisted upon his ten thousand *in advance.* The typical nickel and dime bookie of this era would not see this much money in his lifetime. Chick Gandil

---

50    "Bright's Disease." http:en.wikopedia.org/wike/Bright%27s_disease. 1. Accessed 15 April, 2006.

had the difficult task of shopping for a large sum of money and maintaining relative secrecy at the same time.

It would soon become apparent that if the Black Sox would sell a World Series there were buyers in the market. At least three such investment groups would come forth. Gandil knew of a man with the kind of connections to make such a bargain. Joseph "Sport" Sullivan was a bookmaker and a gambler.[51] Gandil and Sullivan had "done business" when Chick had played for the Washington Senators from 1912 to 1917. Sport would assure Gandil that such a scheme was possible. Sullivan would later admit that his concern was more that of the immorality of tampering with a World Series than the possibilities of punishment if discovered.[52] Apparently Sullivan had noted the track record. Major league baseball players had gotten away with this type of scam on numerous occasions.

Former major league pitcher William "Sleepy Bill" Burns had retired and entered the oil business. Burns contacted Cicotte as rumors surfaced that something was amiss. Burns and his partner Billy Maharg wanted in on the "action."[53] These two men had a significant problem as far as the ballplayers were concerned- they were under financed.

The real "pros" of the gambling business were a bit more cautious. Arnold Rothstein "The Fixer" was not sure that the scheme had any value at all.[54] When originally approached by Bill Maharg and Bill Burns approached Rothstein with the plan at a New York race track Rothstein was cool to the idea. AR would later tell Burns that in his opinion "whatever that was worth"[55] the plan was unworkable. The opinion of "The Big Bankroll" was

51   Eliot Asinof, *EIGHT MEN OUT.* (New York: Harry Holt and Company,1963), 6.
52   Ibid. 9.
53   Ibid. 23.
54   Ibid. 29.
55   Ibid. 29.

worth a lot. The "movers and shakers" in the gambling business often sought AR's opinion. His savvy as to what was a workable scheme had long been appreciated. The theory that one needs to have money to make money is not a new one. Arnold Rothstein's judgment in matters of gambling had been sound for years and would remain so for several more. Those of lesser expertise had come to the proper source for an expert opinion.

On January 17, 1882 Arnold Rothstein was born in New York City. Abraham and Ester Rothstein his parents were honest, hard working folks. Their son Arnold's love for money, especially "easy" and often illegal was reported to have caused a permanent family rift. If moving on without the blessing of his parents was a regret of the gambler, he must have kept the matter well hidden. The younger Rothstein had "worlds to conquer." The allure of money can sometimes overcome many sorrows.

In 1904 AR met Abe Attel on a trip to Saratoga Springs, New York.[56] Arnold took a liking to "the Little Champ." Rothstein enjoyed the "boxing connection" and Abe's company. Attel had been a magnificent featherweight boxer who had held the world title in that division for twelve years. It is reported that Attel fought three hundred sixty five times as a pro and lost only six matches.[57] Upon retirement from his athletic career Abe had accomplished little outside of the gambling world. Rothstein employed Abe as a "bodyguard and errand boy." It is a good thing that "The Big Bankroll" liked Attel; Some of Abe's actions during the 1919 World Series could have caused Abe some very unfortunate consequences had AR become seriously angered.

In August of 1909 Arnold had pawned his wife's jewelry and borrowed $2,000.00 from his father-in-law to open a gambling

---

56    "An Arnold Rothstein Chronology." http://www.davidpietrusza.com/
      Rothstein-Chronology.html. 1. Accessed 9 October, 2005.
57    "The Major Players." available from http://www/blackbetsy.com/jjmajor.
      html. 1. Accessed 4 December, 2004.

house.[58] AR, it would seem, had "the guts of a cat burglar." By 1913 Rothstein's annual income had reached $300,000. In the intervening years Rothstein had learned the value of political connections. This lesson was priceless in his illegal occupation. His friendship with "Tammany Hall" leader Charles Francis Murphy would greatly increase his influence in the city.[59] AR was learning to "cover his bases" better than a rookie second baseman.

By 1914 not only was "The man uptown" laying off bets for fellow gamblers, he had ventured into the real estate and insurance businesses.[60] Rothstein was a visionary. This imaginative approach extended to both sides of the law. AR was in a rough business. He understood early that the best survivors were not the "muscle" but rather the financiers. Rothstein would make a fortune with illegal gambling operations. The public, apparently, wanted to gamble- that the process was against the law only added to the profits of those willing to take risks.

Arnold found his real "gold mine" in prohibition. The American public *would not stop drinking*. Arnold used his big bankroll to finance production and distribution of liquor on both sides of the Atlantic. Some have believed that obtaining illegal income, sheltering those funds behind legitimate business, paying taxes for the business and shielding the illegal income by that obtained within the law was a concept of the late Twentieth Century. If the Mafia perfected the structure, Arnold Rothstein drew the blueprint. One might pause to wonder if Alphonse Capone might have had better success in his relationship with the federal government some years later had Rothstein been available to "cook his books" in the place of Jake "Greasy Thumb" Gusik. At the time of his death Arnold Rothstein was not only a legendary mobster, he was fabulously rich.

His friend, Abe Attell would eventually lure Arnold into the

---

58    "An Arnold Rothstein Chronology." Accessed 9 October, 2005. 1.
59    Ibid. 10 October, 2005.
60    Ibid.

financing plan. Attell began the plot by contacting Burns and Maharg indicating that Rothstein had "changed his mind." and the plan would go forward. Attell must have been close to "the Big Bankroll," it is rumored than men had been killed for less deceit. Rothstein's expertise would play a significant part in the later portions of the story.

In the "pre television" era of baseball, playing fields were not custom designed to the wishes of a franchise. Owners purchased land that they could afford. The ballparks were built around existing structures. It was not until many years later that a team could afford to purchase massive acreage and build to the wishes of team ownership. These logistical problems prevented "cookie cutter" stadiums. Later facilities were usually designed symmetrically. The foul lines were equidistant. Center field was about four hundred feet from home plate. Most important, there were no obstructed views of the action on the field. Such stadiums were all in the future of major league baseball. The construction of early ballparks was based upon different circumstances. In spite of the obstacles, some of the "classic" baseball structures were built during the era of the Black Sox.

Recent baseball historians have marveled that sports fans enjoy the experience of an event held in Boston's Fenway Park or Chicago's Wrigley Field more than journeys to much more modern facilities. These stadiums are the sole survivors of legendary facilities including the Polo Grounds in New York, Ebbets Field in Brooklyn, Forbes Field in Pittsburgh, Municipal Stadium in Cleveland and many others. The nuances of each of these ball yards made each game into an adventure. The 1919 World Series was held in two such venues.

The Series would begin at Redland Field in Cincinnati. The structure was completed in time for a baseball opening April 11, 1912.[61] The park would remain the home of the Reds until 1970.

---

[61]  "Crosley Field, a. k. a. Redland Field." http://www.baseball-statistics. com/Ballparks/Cin/Crosley.htm. 1. Accessed 5 October, 2005.

After Powell Crosley Jr. purchased the Cincinnati Reds in 1934 the name of the facility was changed to "Crosley Field" presumably to advertise the refrigerators, radios and automobiles that the new owner produced.[62].

Crosley Field was a comfortable little playing field. At peak the seating capacity of the facility was only 29,488. The Reds would abandon their old home in 1970 for the modern Three Rivers Stadium. In the interim Redlands Field housed some magnificent moments. The 1919 World Series was among them.

By the time of the start of Game One of the World Series on October 1, 1919 those allegedly acting on behalf of Arnold Rothstein had completed financial arrangements. Eddie Cicotte had received his ten thousand dollars "in advance." The distribution of payments throughout the remainder of the Series would be a point of contention between the players and the gamblers. It does not seem surprising that trust and good will did not abound between two such "honorable" groups.

There were those who once believed that it would be impossible to control the outcome of a major league baseball game. It seemed that there were just too many possibilities and there was too little control of where the ball would go. This theory was forever put to rest in 1919. There was a prearranged signal from the players to Rothstein that "the deal" was to go forth. As with just about every other aspect of "the Fix" even this simple act would not be flawless. It took two tries for the players to tell "the money" that their intentions were, indeed, dishonorable.

---

[62]   Ibid. 4.

# CHAPTER FIVE

It is ironic that Eddie could not immediately perform such a simple task. He was, after all, the best hurler on the White Sox' staff. While few considered him the very "best" of his era (that title might have gone to Walter Johnson, Mathewson or a select few others) Cicotte was certainly near the top of this list. One major reason why Chicago was such a heavy favorite was "pitching." In game one Cincinnati would send left handed Walter "Dutch" Ruether. This hurler had considerable skill. Later in his career Ruether would be the "fourth" starting pitcher with the 1927 New York Yankees. That team is always mentioned as among the greatest in baseball history. Dutch would pitch over twenty one hundred big league innings and accumulate one hundred thirty seven wins.[63] In 1919 Ruether compiled what could be seen as his best year. His nineteen wins were accompanied by only six losses. The "seven sixty" winning percentage was one hundred seventy nine points higher than his lifetime mark. In spite of all that the Reds'starter had accomplished in 1919, few gave him a chance against the legendary Cicotte in Game One.

Before Eddie Cicotte could do anything to affect the outcome of the game, Dutch had to "try his luck. " The White Sox had an advantage in the first "at bats" of the Series. Each of the hitters who would swing in this frame was trying to win. Shano singled to center to begin the game. Cocky attempted to sacrifice, but Ruether fielded it cleanly and fired to Larry Kopf, covering second to retire the lead runner. E. Collins such an accomplished base runner that he would steal seven hundred forty one "regular season" bases in nine hundred fourteen attempts for a fine .811

---

[63]    "Dutch Reuther" available from http.www.baseball library.com. Accessed September 17, 2005. 1.

percentage[64] then tried to steal second. The man who may well have been second only to Ty Cobb in theft ability during the era was retired. Wingo fired to Morrie Rath just in time to nip the runner. Weaver's fly to Big Edd was caught in left center. "Rousch raced over from center and made a remarkable catch retiring the side."[65]

Eddie Cicotte had two favorite pitches in his repertoire: the spitball (now illegal) and the knuckleball. Both of these servings are legendary as being hard to control. No one would be expected to notice if one of these offerings would "get away" from Cicotte. With this cover, Cicotte went ahead and hit Cincinnati leadoff hitter Maurice Rath with that second pitch in the initial turn at bat for the Reds in the bottom of the first inning of the opening game.[66] On the first pitch Morrie showed the reflexes and dexterity of a professional athlete, eluding a Cicotte spitball aimed at his head. Knuckles was throwing at a rather small target. Rath stood only five feet eight inches tall and weighed no more than one hundred sixty pounds.[67] Eddie wouldn't continue in his frustration for long.

The right-hander wouldn't miss twice. Pitch number two was a fastball, "plunking" Rath squarely in the middle of the back. It is believed that "Knuckles" had deliberately chosen the fastball.[68] Eddie probably wanted the pitch to hurt. In spite of the money, Eddie may have been humiliated and confused of his own feelings. Poor Morrie was merely on the receiving end of the hurler's

64 "Eddie Collins." *THE BASEBALL E.NCYCLOPEDIA.* Edited by Gary Gillette and Peter Palmer. Barnes and Noble Books. New York. 2004.

65 "1919 World Series Game 1." available from http://www.blackbetsy. com/19game1.htm. Accessed 4 December, 2004.

66 "Edward V. Cicotte" available from http: www.1919blacksox.com; accessed December 3, 2004. 1.

67 "Maurice Rath." available from http://www.baseballlibrary.com/baseballlibrary/ballplayers/R/Rath_Maurice.stm. Accessed 21 October, 2005. 1.

68 Asinof, *EIGHT MEN OUT.* 64

frustrations. Make no mistake about it, being hit in the middle of the back with a baseball is a "breathtaking experience." In a way Rath was lucky, Eddie didn't intend to do him any permanent harm. A more vindictive man would have aimed the pitch at the back of Morrie's neck. The real "head hunters" often did that. In the portion of a second that the batter has to ascertain that the ball is headed for his cranium, the instinctive reaction is to back away from the plate, the area of perceived danger. This instinctive move often brings the head into the perfect position to collide with the ball. The Cincinnati second baseman had to face no such terror. In addition Cicotte could not throw with the velocity of a Walter Johnson or later a Dizzy Dean, Bob Feller or Sandy Koufax. These gentlemen could probably have hit a player in the back and had the object exit from the player's chest. Eddie didn't throw anywhere near that hard. Rath survived, was not seriously injured and continued in the game. His back was, however, probably "seriously sore" for several days. Most important, Cicotte had delivered his answer to Rothstein. The deal was sealed.

The Reds would score but one run in that first inning.[69] Whether the hit that Jake Daubert as achieved as he followed Rath to the plate or Heinie Groh's sacrifice fly moments later to score the run were "Cicotte aided" is impossible to determine. The Reds were a pennant winning ball club and could do some things right. Had the Reds realized what a bonanza they had stumbled upon, the inning could have been much worse. Daubert tried to move up to second as Rath was scoring. As the play at the plate failed, Schalk fired to Risberg, who held onto the ball, in time to retire Jake. This out would be critical as Rousch walked before Duncan grounded out to end the frame. Who knows how much more damage the home team could have done with the benefit of an extra out had Jake merely held his station on Heinie's fly.

---

[69] http//www/blaclbetsy.com//19game 1.htm Page 1. Accessed 4 December 2004.

This is a particularly interesting question given Cicotte's pitiful pitching performance in the entire game. Was Eddie desperate enough to groove one to Larry Kopf who would have come to the plate given that "extra out"? In that case, the first inning could have lasted for a long time.

In the overall picture of this World Series this inning was a small thing. If anyone ever asked Eddie Cicotte of the specific incidents of this inning, it did not appear in my research. Perhaps it only made a difference as to degree of guilt. Nothing serious had been lost in this first inning. To all of the world it seemed as though this one run margin would be almost nothing for the powerful White Sox to overcome.

There were those who once believed that baseball games could not be "fixed." The game contained too many variables to allow individual ballplayers to manipulate the outcome. Professional ballplayers had proven this wrong in the past and would, unfortunately, do so again. Some basis for this theory was, however, seen in the second inning of this very same game. Two of the "Black Sox," supposedly trying to lose the game, were involved in the first Chicago run. Joe Jackson hit a routine ground ball to Cincinnati shortstop Larry Kopf. Kopf muffed the play then threw wildly. Jackson wound up safe at second on the play. Kopf was charged with an error. Gandil followed by hitting a "blooper" into left field which Rousch was unable to get to after a long run. Jackson scored, the game was tied and Jackson and Gandil were heroes for a moment. Baseball is a strange game. It is questionable as to whether either Jackson or Gandil had intended to succeed. While is likely that Joe was trying harder than Chick (Jackson would later maintain his own innocence) the confusion of all that was happening at once could distract from the concentration of even "the greatest natural hitter who ever lived." Whatever the circumstances, the "Black Sox" had put the White Sox even. The combination of events had, however, made Eddie Cicotte's daunting task even more formidable.

At some time in the early innings of Game One it must have occurred to Eddie Cicotte that his fellow conspirators were placing the responsibility for this loss entirely upon his shoulders. Eddie had not "hatched" the plot. He was not even a vindictive participant; this role was much better suited to Gandil or Risberg. Cicotte's quandary was a matter of economics. All of the players were expecting to negotiate new contracts for the next season. None of them wanted to look bad enough to endanger the success of these proceedings. Could the other players have helped but rationalizing that their roles could be small? Perhaps the losses could be manipulated entirely by Cicotte and Williams. Perhaps none of the rest had looked far enough to consider Williams' next start. This day they would be content to have the burden all fall upon "Knuckles." After all, Eddie had received his money "up front."

The bottom half of the second inning would not add to the drama. Larry Kopf struck out. Greasy Neale grounded out to Cocky and Ivy Wingo stroked a routine fly to Happy Felsch in center field. Chicago sustained no damage in the second. "No damage" would become the best that the Sox could hope for during the entire Series. Cicotte could have taken some small consolation from this inning. While he had not pitched to the "heart" of the Cincinnati order, the veteran right handed hurler could still get big league hitters out when he wanted to. It is doubtful that the little boy growing up in Michigan could have ever imagined that the "want to" would ever disappear

The third was a "draw" with no advantage to either team. In the "top half" Cicotte began by striking out. It would not be expected that Eddie would be able to connect with Ruether's servings on a consistent basis. A good hitting pitcher is a rare commodity. Perhaps it is the development of different muscles concerned with throwing or swinging. It could be a lack of concentration, the time spent away from the "hill" is used by the hurler to plan his next ascent to that area. Perhaps the timing of a swing is lost during the days in between starts. There are many theories regarding the lack of "hitting pitchers. Whatever the logic, Cicotte was not among those chosen few who could handle both tasks with success. To his credit Cicotte had become a "master" at the skill he had chosen to develop. Unfortunately, he was offensive help upon this occasion. No one else was either. Shano flied to Rousch and Eddie Collins stroked a routine ground ball and was retired Kopf to Daubert (shortstop to first base.)

The Reds fared slightly better in their half of the frame. Dutch Ruether drew a walk leading off. Morrie Rath dribbled a grounder along the first base line and was retired Cicotte to Gandil. The affect was the same as a sacrifice as Ruether moved up to second base. That was as far as Dutch would get. Both Daubert and Groh "skied" out to Jackson in left.[70]

The visitor's half of the fourth inning was also uneventful. Bucky tried to bunt down the third base line. Groh threw him out easily. Jackson tapped out to Kopf. Kopf also handled a much harder stroked grounder by Felsch and again threw to Daubert for the out.

Installment one of Cicotte's "bill" was paid in the Cincinnati fourth inning. Happy loped into deep left center field to bring down Edd Roush's long drive. While it is not recorded what the pitcher might have thought at this point, it is apparent that he received no help on that one. Pat Duncan lined a single to right field. Eddie Collins then made an artful stop of a vicious ground ball off the bat of Larry Kopf. E. Collins fired to Risberg in an effort to start what appeared to be a "tailor made" double play. The shortstop bobbled the ball just momentarily. The "force out" at second was successful but The Swede's relay to first failed to "double" Kopf. As a consequence, there were only two outs, the

---

[70]   Ibid. 2. Accessed 4 December 2004.

inning was still alive. [71] Discreet as it may have been, Cicotte's "help" had arrived.

The rest of this inning reads similar to a scene from "The Bad News Bears." Kopf moved to second as Greasy Neale hit a ground single to short that Risberg knocked down but could not make a play on. "Inches" between handling a ball cleanly and just knocking it down. "Fractions of a second" between a strong throw to retire a runner and an average peg that barely missed the put out. While Risberg was a genius at these types of distinctions, it is often difficult to tell which of his actions were carefully calculated and which were not designed. It is not surprising that Charles August Risberg was always strangely silent on this subject.

Alfred Earle "Greasy" Neale was a multitalented and very interesting individual. Not only would Neale fashion an eight year career in major league baseball, this was only the beginning of Greasy's presence upon the athletic stage. Baseball would be but a sideshow of this man's talents. Neale would build a Hall of Fame career as a football player and later as a coach. Athletes of this era were often noted for their versatility. Jim Thorpe was voted as the greatest American athlete of the first half of the twentieth century in a *SPORT MAGIZINE* poll. Thorpe was a magnificent track and football athlete. Jim also played major league baseball for six years contributing a career batting average of only .252. This statistic is very similar to Neale's career mark of .259 over an eight year span. Standing alone, these performances would not be outstanding. Many observers believe that hitting a moving baseball is the single most difficult task in sports. Few could master this art while dividing time with other physical activities. This is why multi sport athletes such as Neale, Thorpe and Bo Jackson (a magnificent football and baseball star of the 1980s and 1990s

---

[71]    "The 1919 World Series Play By Play Game 1' available from http// www.blackbetsy.com/19game1.htm,2.

who had his career tragically shortened by a horrible knee injury) are held in such high esteem.

On the next play Ivey Wingo singled to right, scoring Kopf who just "outran" Shano's throw to the plate and Neale moved on to third. Ruether tripled, scoring both Neale and Wingo. Unlike Cicotte, Ruether had helped his own cause considerably. The agony was not yet over. Rath singled, Daubert doubled and Gleason had seen enough. The White Sox skipper replaced Cicotte with Roy Wilkinson but the damage had been done. [72] A six to one deficit was not insurmountable. ChiSox fans had seen their team rally from worse predicaments at times in the past. "All was not lost." Baseball fans are incurable optimists. The players on both teams may have already sensed the finality of the fourth inning rally.

Gandil led off the White Sox fifth inning with a single. Chick may have correctly believed that little damage could be done by one hit at this point. Risberg threatened a bunt and chopped a line drive to Rousch. The center fielder had no problem handling this one and Gandil had no chance to advance, even had he wanted to. Groh grabbed Schalk's grounder and fired to Rath to force Gandil. Wilkinson grounded to Rath who stepped on the second base bag to force Schalk. The Sox had done no damage to Reuther and the Reds. [73]

In the Cincinnati half of the inning Felsch was "bothered by the sun"[74] on a fly ball off the bat of Rousch but made the catch. That big yellow object in the sky is always a factor in day time baseball games. The most experienced players often have to "duck and cover" to protect themselves from the harm of a fly ball. This happens to the most experienced and capable outfielders. Oscar was among the best. This time he recovered in time to make the play. Happy may have also determined that the game was "out of

---

[72] Ibid.
[73] Ibid.
[74] Ibid.

hand" and it was, finally, time to play baseball. Pat Duncan, one of the heroes of the previous inning singled past Risberg into left center field. Louis Baird "Pat" Duncan was a fine major league hitter. His career batting average over seven years was .307. In the eight games against Chicago in October, 1919 the left fielder hit .269. This game was the high mark of that Series. Apparently, Duncan played better when the entire other team was trying to "win" the games. One more "fool" tried to steal in opposition to Cracker's arm. Duncan was deprived of theft from Schalk to Risberg.

The Swede made "the best play of the game"[75] behind second to grab Kopf's smash and throw him out to Gandil.

The rest of the game was "academic. " The home team scored two runs in their seventh inning opposing Wilkinson and added one in the last of the eighth off of Grover Lowdermilk. Unless one was betting the spread and who knows, some may have been, it made no difference at all. The Cincinnati Reds won game one easily. 9-1

---

[75]  Ibid.

# CHAPTER SIX

It has been widely reported that "things did not go well" among the White Sox personnel between games one and two. It seems that a frustrated Ray Schalk exchanged pleasantries with Eddie Cicotte beneath the stands of Cincinnati's Redland Field. [76] Perhaps Cracker was merely showing Knuckles a few wrestling moves and boxing maneuvers that he had picked up in his youth, but given the mental outlooks that the two must have assumed after the game it is doubtful that that was the case. Later it is said that manager Kid Gleason exchanged words with Risberg in the hotel lobby after the game. [77] The skipper probably did not compliment the shortstop on his fine work in the game earlier. Gleason loved baseball. It must have been clear to him at this point that the rumors were true. The panic of being tied to the railroad tracks as the train was approaching must have set in. It is almost certain that Gleason could not believe the circumstances that he and his team had become involved in. Fortunately, the Kid knew he was too old for sparring, But still he lashed out at the nearest available antagonist.

Schalk could not believe that Cicotte could not control any of his pitches, his legendary spitball, knuckleball or better than average fastball any better than he had in the initial game. Cracker grumbled that Eddie had been "crossing him up." throwing pitches other than those called for by the catcher, in the initial game. Nothing had happen that could be proven as deliberate, but the diminutive catcher "knew." During the baseball season a catcher might well be closer to his pitching staff than to his wife. Certainly Cracker spent more time with the hurlers than he did at home. Infidelity hurts! The diminutive catcher had been

---

[76]   CHICAGO BLACK SOX.. available from www.chs.org/history/blacksox/blk4.html. 2.

[77]   Asimof, EIGHT MEN OUT, 72.

"cheated upon." He could only dream that the differences could still be reconciled.

Claude Williams had a problem as he prepared to face Harry "Slim" Salee and the Reds in Game Two. In the midst of all of the turmoil about him, he had to keep his head. Lefty had to appear as though he wanted to win and still lose the game. Williams had to be a much better actor than Cicotte had been in the previous game. It is much easier to attempt to win a ballgame than to try to lose one. Those who are competing at their best expect to win but "sometimes the bear gets you." It can be madding to use all of one's individual skills merely to find out that on one given day the opposition was just a little bit better. Such pressure had driven such great players as "Big Ed" Delahanty to walk off of a train track into a raging river and fall to death less than a decade before. Delahanty's end would be much more tragic than that of Williams. Lefty would live to face another day. Still, Claude must have wondered, how does one let the bear get his meal with so many suspicious eyes looking on? To complicate matters considerably, in 1919 "Slim" Salee, "the honorable opponent" had not been "half bad."

Salee had a long but rather unspectacular career as a major league hurler. While winning One hundred seventy four games over fourteen years, he lost slightly less times: one hundred and forty three. This "average" record of 12.4 wins and 10.1 losses per year becomes even less impressive when one disregards Sallee's 21-7 performance of 1919. Clearly, Cincinnati had seen his "the chance of a lifetime" year in 1919. Would the Sox see this impressive pitcher or the ordinary one who had toiled for the Cardinals and Giants in prior years? How would Sallee's career mediocrity or recent brilliant efforts affect the efforts of some Sox to win the game or the exploits of others to lose the contest? No wonder AR had "bet the Series." It was clear that "heaven" or some other entity needed to help those who had wagered upon the individual games.

Eddie Cicotte's performance in the first game had been so pitiful that many close to the game "smelled a rat." If Williams allowed a repetition of such a fiasco Kid Gleason would have to do something. Roy Wilkinson and Bill James would not normally be options in the White Sox pitching rotation. Either of these individuals could, however, lift their arms and throw a baseball sixty feet six inches across the plate. No one would ever speak of these hurlers as "stars. " The two "workmanlike" performers had not played critical roles in the ascent to the World Series of the Chicago White Sox. These men, nonetheless, could be used if the Sox manager became so desperate as to decide to abandon the hurlers who had won a pennant on Chicago's south side. This dilemma was further complicated by the fact that Sallee, working on behalf of the opposition, was a capable pitcher at the conclusion of his outstanding "career"season. Williams needed to pitch badly enough to lose- just barely.

John "Shano" Collins opened the game by grounding out pitcher to first base (Salee to Jake Daubert.) Cocky worked the Reds' hurler for a walk. Bucky smashed a line drive to Larry Kopf. It is sometimes said that if a baseball had been hit one foot in any different direction (left, right, up or down) it would have been a hit. No one could have blamed Weaver had he mumbled something about that as he tossed his bat aside. A moment too late Eddie Collins realized the drive would not clear the Reds' infield. E. Collins was doubled easily on Kopf's throw to Daubert at first. In this case the fine reflexes and quickness that had made the second baseman a great player had done the Chicago club "in." A slower player would not have had time to stray far enough to be "doubled up" by Kopf's peg. The Sox had done no damage to begin the game.

In the years subsequent to this World Series the various loyalties of the Black Sox have been constantly questioned. The intrigue and contradictions of this particular sequence of baseball proved that these inquiries were founded with good reason.

Claude Williams' problem of allegiance was greatly magnified in game two. If Cicotte had twirled a two hit shutout in Game One Williams may have been willing to scrap all of the plans of ill begotten riches and played to win in Game Two. This had not happened. Eddie's "neck" was already "on the line." It was no longer a mere matter of money. Now six other players were in the same boat as Knuckles. Williams must have considered the number of players on his entire team to be eight. They had cemented a deal with the gamblers. What kind of man would Lefty have been had he chosen to leave his friend "to swing alone"?

The actions of his other friends, specifically Gandil and Risberg showed that they too were complicit in the conspiracy. The division of payment the night before had been the mortar for everyone, save Weaver. The left handed pitcher was loyal to the White Sox. His efforts to the conclusion of the 1920 season would reflect that sentiment. Williams' actions would indicate that he was even more "beholding" to Cicotte and his other six friends. Perhaps knowing that the die had already been cast, Lefty would pitch of dedication to his portion of the team more than to that of the entire unit. This was a burden that Lefty Williams would bear at great price.

Maurice Rath used his diminutive size and good "batting eye" to work the count full to lead off the bottom of the first. The "lack of punch in Morrie's bat" was displayed as he stroked a lazy fly ball that Felsch handled easily in center field.[78] Jake Daubert dribbled a gentle grounder to the Swede. Risberg threw Jake out easily.[79] Groh lined out to Shano Collins and the first inning was over.

Sallee counted on Joe Jackson taking the first pitch in the second inning. Slim guessed right. The fastball was strike one. Had the slugger been swinging, the hurler's serving would have

---

[78] THE 1919 WORLD SERIES PLAY BY PLAY GAME TWO. Available from http://www.blackbetsy.com. 1. Accessed 4 December, 2004.

[79] Ibid. Accessed 4. December, 2004.

probably been no match for the swing of one of the greatest hitters who ever lived. Baseball is often just "a game of minds." The second pitch may not have been Joe's best swing either. Jackson blooped a short fly behind second, just out of the reach of both Rousch and Duncan. The double would "look like a line drive" in the box score. The newspapers had given baseball to the masses of the American public but the feeling "of" the game could not be committed to paper. By the time the ball was retrieved, Joe was at second base. Happy sacrificed Jackson to third but he was stranded there as Gandil grounded to Kopf and Risberg skied to Neale. Perhaps Chick and the Swede felt that it was too early to take the lead. Perhaps Sallee had just "gotten them out," or perhaps no one will ever really know exactly what was happening While baseball teams use a variety of signs during a game, there are probably none for "do we take 'a dive' now or later?"

Big Edd Rousch led off the Reds'half of the second by drawing a "free pass." It is not known if this move was intentional. Even great pitchers often saw the wisdom of "pitching around" the Reds' center fielder. It was often wiser to give this man first base and take the chance of retiring lesser hitters than to run the risk of Rousch banging a "long ball" and having his opposition fall behind with one swing of Rousch's big bat.

The strategy worked well in this circumstance. Rousch would advance no further than first base. Pat Duncan, the next scheduled Cincinnati hitter, lined "a scorching drive"[80] to E. Collins. Eddie fired to Chick Gandil at first in time to double Rousch for the first two outs of the inning. Kopf flied to Happy Felsch and the inning was over.

Schalk lined to Edd Rousch for the first out of the Sox' third. Williams lined a single to center field. It seems that those who assert that "the game was better back then…" have an argument in asserting that there were, over the years surrounding this World

---

80    Ibid.

Series, many pitchers who were good hitters. Later, the American League would change the rules such that pitchers would not hit at all. Even in the "Senior Circuit" of the National League good hitting pitchers were few and far between. Many teams of the "Dead Ball" era of baseball sent nine hitters to the plate in their lineup. In this case the hurler did better than the two subsequent batsmen. Shano flied out to Duncan and Eddie grounded unassisted to Daubert to conclude the half inning.

Greasy Neale struck out to begin the Reds' half. Raridan lifted a fly to Jackson in left-center and Salee popped to Weaver. Thus far Slim had been less help with the bat than his counterpart. Pitchers are, after all, athletes. Comparisons between the complete efforts of the players are inevitable. As a team, Cincinnati had been fruitless in their third.

Buck singled to center on Sallee's first serving in the fourth inning.[81] Jackson singled to left. Happy laid down a sacrifice bunt fielded by Sallee who tossed to Rath covering first. This was a fundamental baseball play that Felsch had executed perfectly. Many games have been lost due to the failure to complete such basic maneuvers. With runners on second and third and only one out it appeared that the Sox were "in business." To the Chicago fans it was the right idea, but the wrong hitters. Gandil bounded meekly to Kopf who fired to Raridan. The throw had Weaver by "twelve feet."[82] The only way Bucky could have scored was if the Reds' catcher had dropped the ball. Raridan was too good with the glove to allow this to happen often. Bill "hung on" and Weaver was out. The outcome of Risberg's "at bat" was a forgone conclusion. The Swede popped to Daubert at first and the White Sox had wasted a marvelous opportunity.

The first three and one half innings had been scoreless. The Chicago fans may have begun to feel that the nightmare of the

---

81    Ibid.
82    Ibid. 2.

day before was behind them. They were wrong. Morrie Rath led off the Cincinnati fourth by drawing a base on balls. Jake Daubert sacrificed the runner to second. Groh walked. Edd Roush singled to center to score Rath. Later in the same frame Pat Duncan drew a base on balls and Larry Kopf tripled to score two more runs. The result of the inning was that the Reds had three runs on only two hits.[83] In the "pre home run" era of baseball, teams seldom scored more runs in an inning than they accumulated hits. In such innings the offensive output was always aided by the "letdowns" of the defensive unit. This certainly had been the case for the Reds. The damage would have been much less severe had Williams not issued "free passes" to Rath, Groh and Duncan. Close observation would indicate that the Cincinnati rally had been more to the fault of Williams than to the credit of the Reds. It doesn't take "much" to turn the tide of a major league baseball game.

After the fourth inning Lefty Williams was again brilliant. The Reds scored but one more run the rest of the game. The Cincinnati pitching was just as solid. Either "Slim" was at his best or the "Black Sox" were at their worse. After the fourth there never seemed to be a sense that Chicago was "in" the game. The Sox did get two runs in their seventh inning. After Gandil rolled out, Daubert to Sallee covering first, the Swede singled to left field. Cracker followed with a sharp double down the right field line. Neale fired to second but his throw eluded both Rath and Kopf. Heinie Groh would normally have been in position to back up his teammates. This was not possible as the third sacker had retreated to the bag for a possible play there. The throw wound up in foul territory behind third and Chicago had two runs. Chicago could get no closer. Lefty (no pinch hitter?) struck out and Shano flied to Rousch in center to end the rally.

---

[83]  *THE 1919 WORLD SERIES PLAY BY PLAY GAME TWO* . Available from http://blackby.com/19game 2. Accessed 4 December, 2004.

John Collins managed a single in the eighth and Gandil and Schalk sandwiched singles around a Risberg double play in the ninth. This action was inconsequential. Cincinnati had beaten Chicago again.

Those who favored the ChiSox could take some consolation in the fact that their team was never "out" of this ballgame. "Close" however "counts only in horseshoes and hand grenades."[84] The White Sox had shown slight signs of life, but were on the short end of a 4-2 score. Comiskey, Gleason and Schalk may not have been fooled by the performance. Reuther and Sallee were not such great pitchers to stop the opponents so completely in consecutive games. Those closest to the team may have "smelled a rat" but many of those in the rest of the world thought it was an outstanding effort on the part of the underdog. The most loyal White Sox fans were not ready to panic. But for one sour inning and a couple of "bad breaks" the win would have belonged to Chicago.

The beauty of Claude Williams' misguided effort can only emphasize the remarkable skills of professional athletes in general and baseball players in particular. In football an offensive tackle blocks a defensive end. On the same play the guard knocks down the linebacker creating a gap for an outstanding run by a fullback. The result is a "sight to behold." On this play there was some room for adjustment by each of the offensive participants. A baseball pitcher has no such margin for error. The difference of a few inches in location or a few miles per hour in velocity can turn a perfect pitch into one that has "double written all over it."

Cicotte had not fooled Ray Schalk. Lefty had no better success. A catcher is the nerve center of a baseball team. After many years of catching White Sox hurlers Cracker knew them well. Ray was alert enough to watch Lefty more carefully than most. When

---

84    unknown.

Claude's performance was pathetic Schalk was waiting under the stands for him as well. This time the discussion deteriorated into exchanged punches.[85] Most of these were delivered by the catcher. Later, to save the morale of the team, Schalk apologized. There should have been no need. It is ironic that a man giving everything he had to win for his ball club would need ask forgiveness from those who were trying to lose. Schalk was the ultimate team player, hoping for a miracle to pull his team through. In the end, the gesture was of no use. The words must have "stuck in the throat" of the little catcher. The fruitlessness of attempting to avert this "train wreck" was all too obvious. While it would bring him little consolation in his later life, the catcher could draw some solace in the mere fact that: "Cracker was right!"

---

[85] Asinof. *EIGHT MEN OUT.* 90.

# CHAPTER SEVEN

The fans of the White Sox could see that the team was not in an ideal situation. Still, trailing two games to none in a nine game series was not an insurmountable obstacle. The Chicago backers felt that they had a far superior team. In addition, the club was headed "home." Most teams play much better at the park they call "their own." Familiarity with the physical surroundings of the field is a factor. Perhaps much more important, the routine of the season is much more settled when the athletes can "sleep in their own bed and eat home cooking." Many little distractions such as transportation to and from the park, scheduled eating time, laundry and filling the endless free hours between games are taken care of on the first home stand of the season. With these details taken care of the player's mind is much more focused upon the game of the day.

In 1919 the White Sox playing field was Comiskey Park. This facility erected in 1910 should not be confused with the new "US Cellular Field" built in the late Twentieth Century. The purchase of naming rights for a stadium was a concept unheard of in 1910. For a time in the 1970s the park carried the moniker "White Sox Park" as new ownership attempted to distance the operation from the Comiskey family. When Bill Veeck purchased the team late in that decade he said simply "It's Comiskey Park, the old man built it and it should have his name on it." We agree with Veeck. There should be no confusion in this work: the place was "Comiskey Park."

When it was completed in 1910 Comiskey Park was considered a magnificent new structure. The stadium replaced South Side Park which had become obsolete with the building of new concrete and steel facilities. The original seating capacity was for thirty two thousand patrons. The cost at construction was $750,000. The park was designed to "last forever." Charlie

Comiskey would not put up that much of his own money (privately financed, no public money) to build garbage. The seating capacity was expanded to fifty two thousand in 1927. Later customer accommodations would place the seats available at the time of destruction at 43,951.[86]

Considered a wondrous new ballpark at the time of the 1919 World Series, Comiskey Park would retain its magic during its entire existence. It was still fun to watch a game there, as this author did, more than sixty years later. Charlie Comiskey didn't build "junk."

Figures such as seating capacity are very important to the management of a team. This was particularly important to a club in the early part of the 20th Century before radio, television and advertising revenue diminished the value of each "person in a seat." Generally all of these income factors were of little concern to the player of 1919. The concern of the participants in each game was "the field itself."

The playing field on "Chicago's south side" made Comiskey Park a "big ballpark." It was three hundred forty seven feet from home plate to the foul poles in left and right field. The area that would some day be known as "power alleys" in left-center and right center field were three hundred eighty two feet from the plate. The center field fence was a four hundred forty foot shot from the plate. Happy Felsch had as much room as he needed to run down fly balls in the middle of such an area. Nemo Leibold, Shano Collins, Joe Jackson and the rest had to be "on their toes" to handle drives in the corners of such an outfield as well. Those with less practice with the nuances of the outfield area were at a significant disadvantage on the surface of Comiskey Park. "Returning home" should, indeed, be a massive advantage to the White Sox.

---

[86]   http://www.baseball-statistics.com/Ballparks/Chi/WS/Comiskey.htm. 1.
Accessed 6 October, 2005.

An "ugly" thing happened to the Black Sox upon their return to Chicago to prepare for game three of the Series. They didn't get paid the next installment of their "to lose" money. This caused yet another unbelievable twist in a scenario that was rapidly snow-balling out of control. "The Eight" vowed to do there best to get a win for a man they hated, Dickie Kerr. Members of the "Black Sox" portion of the club considered Kerr a "busher" [87](baseball language for "bush league" or not worthy of playing on the major league level-tea.) Two games had been lost for men that these players hoped would be getting bigger contracts the next season and now one would be won for someone that they considered worthy of playing in Newark. What a fascinating group of base-ball players!

As the 1919 baseball season is reviewed, Richard Henry Kerr should be considered the ideal Comiskey employee. His 13-7 record during the regular season was more than satisfactory for a "number four" starter (behind Cicotte, Williams and Faber.) The two wins he amassed in the World Series have always been considered heroic.

Dickie's "strange ride in baseball" was still in its infancy in 1919. In 1920 Kerr was 25-9 in the season that "the scandal" was exposed. In 1921 he was 19-17 for the remnants of a once proud franchise. After that season, he was denied a five hundred dollar raise. Kerr would not sign his contract. Dickie chose to sit out the 1922 season rather than sign for the money Comiskey was offering. As a reward for his insolence, Commissioner Landis suspended Kerr for the 1923 season. The lefty's alleged offense, believe it or not, "associating with gamblers." During the 1922 season Kerr had supplemented his income playing semi pro base-ball. Among those against whom he played: Risberg, Gandil, Jackson, Felsch, Williams and Weaver also trying to scratch out a meager living in the same manner. As further penalty, Kerr was

---

[87]   Asinof, *EIGHT MEN OUT,* 95.

not reinstated in 1924. He spent that season eking out a living pitching for minor league Indianapolis. This was, apparently, to show the all powerful "Czar" of baseball that the diminutive man with the big heart was still a loyal employee of the industry. A seemingly innocent teammate of Kerr's during his semi pro fling was second baseman Darby Rathman of Mount Carmel College. Rathman believed that he had a commitment from the Newark Eagles to continue his playing career when his college eligibility expired. When he concluded his career, the Eagles withdrew their offer. Landis had banned him from organized ball as well. According to Rathman, Landis felt he was doing the second baseman a favor. No one would ever trust Darby after he had participated with the banned players anyway.[88]

After a brief return to the major leagues in the 1925 season, Kerr retired as a player. Baseball was not altogether unkind to Dickie Kerr. He did enjoy a long career as a minor league manager. Hall of Fame ballplayer Stan Musial played in the minors for Kerr. Musial's eldest son Richard was named in honor of Kerr.[89]

As the drama moved back "between the lines" Dickie Kerr needed little help from anyone else on Friday October 3, 1919. Dickie was not an "overpowering" pitcher. His fastball would not intimidate hitters. The pitcher relied on pinpoint control of each serving. Any pitch that was not exactly where Kerr intended it was liable to result in a disaster. The southpaw had to stay one thought ahead of each hitter to have any success at all. It is a testament to the ability of major league hitters to adjust that Kerr's career would last but four seasons. His fifty three major league victories were a comparatively small amount. This is ironic; Kerr certainly had a "Hall of Fame heart!"

The top half of the first inning was "classic Kerr." He induced

---

[88]  http://www.bevillsadvocate.org/histweb/CHAPTER4html. 1. Accessed 8 April, 2006

[89]  http://www.baseballlibrary.com/ballplayers/Kerr_Docloe/st,. 1. Accessed 17 September, 2005.

Maurice Rath to ground out easily from Risberg to Gandil. Daubert hit an easy fly to Felsch and Groh was a rare Kerr strike-out victim.[90]

After his initial at bat in the first inning Nemo Leibold must have wished that Greasy Neale would wander off somewhere with Jim Thorpe to toss a pigskin around. The Sox' outfielder lined a sharp line drive to right that Neale grabbed off of his shoe tops. Leibold was robbed of what appeared to be a sure hit.[91] Eddie Collins bounced out weakly, Fisher to first. Weaver popped to Jake Daubert. [92] Chicago had done no damage in their half of the first.

Kerr tried to sneak a fastball past Rousch leading off the Reds' second. Miraculously, Dickie survived. One of the best hitters of all time may have been over eager. Big Edd bounded to "the Swede" at short. Risberg tossed him out easily. Pat Duncan's blooper over second base fell out of everyone's reach for the Reds' first hit. Kopf's grounder to the Swede looked like an easy double play. Surprise, Risberg hesitated just long enough to avert the opportunity. Perhaps not wanting yet another error on is record, the shortstop recovered in time to throw to Gandil to retire Kopf at first base. Cocky grabbed Neale's grounder and flipped to Chick retiring the side.

Joe Jackson led off the Sox' second with an opposite field single to left. Hap bunted directly to Fisher. Ray fielded it cleanly but then fired over Kopf's head as the shortstop moved to cover second base. Joe scampered to third and Felsch wound up at second base. Chick ripped a single through the "drawn in" infield into right field. Both Jackson and Felsch scored on the play. Gandil hustled into second. If these three players and the rest of "the eight" had played the entire Series in this manner history

---

90    http://www.blackbetsy.com/19game3.htm. 1. Accessed 11 November, 2005.

91    Ibid.

92    Ibid.

might have been entirely different. Weren't the Black Sox trying to "dump" this one? Didn't the Chicago conspirators vow to not win for Kerr? It seems that money, loyalty, hatred and self interest were becoming more and more confused by the minute.

Bill Raridan led off the Reds' half of the third inning.[93] The catcher had been acquired by the Reds from the New York Giants. When Christy Mathewson had "dumped" Hal Chase on the Giants after the "Jimmy Ring incident" Cincinnati had received Raridan. It appears as though the Reds had been twice blessed. They had rid themselves of Hal Chase and acquired a fine backup catcher at the same time.

Unfortunately most of Raridan's notice in baseball would be of the "Fred Merkle and Ralph Branca variety." All three players would amass fine careers. Merkle would be nicknamed "Bonehead" for one play. When he "didn't cover a base," the rival Cubs won a pennant. For years Branca would hold the major league record for wins by a rookie pitcher. No one remembers that. Branca served the ball that allowed Bobby Thomson to hit a playoff ending home run for the New York Giants. The Giants won the pennant on what the press called "the shot heard around the world." There is no record as to what Branca called it.

In a similar fashion, Bill Raridan had been involved in a "run down play" while performing for the 1917 New York Giants. Eddie Collins eluded a tag and sprinted across home plate ahead of the slow footed effort of Heinie Zimmerman to catch him. Zimmerman had to chase Cocky as Raridan had vacated the plate area during the pursuit of Collins. It has always been considered a "major sin" for a player to fail to cover a base *in front of the runner* during a "run down." While Zimmerman was often seen as the "goat" in this matter, baseball experts always blamed Raridan for not being in the proper location at the appropriate moment. Two more good men with stigma attached to their names. The

---

93    Ibid. 2. Accessed 4 December, 2004.

same game that offered "fame and fortune" often brought agony as well.

On Friday October 3, 1919 Raridan would not be in the limelight. Leading off the top half of the Cincinnati third inning Bill grounded weakly to Weaver for the first out of that frame. Kerr intended to let Ray Fisher's dribbler roll foul but slipped and fell on the ball while still in fair territory. Rath popped to Risberg at short and Daubert grounded into a force- Cocky Collins to the Swede. Once again, Kerr was not masterful but the opponent had done no damage.

Eddie Collins led off the Sox portion of the inning with a single off of Larry Kopf's glove. Buck Weaver combined with the second baseman to pull off a perfect hit and run play. Shoeless Joe attempted to sacrifice. As is often the case when a "race horse is asked to pull a plow," the attempt failed. Daubert grabbed Jackson's pop fly just behind the pitcher's mound. Groh snagged Felsch's hot shot at third, fired to Rath at second, on to Daubert. Double play, inning over.

It seems to be an interesting coincidence in baseball that when a player makes a fine defensive play to retire the opposition, that player often leads off the next turn "at bat" for his team. This was the case as Heinie Groh led off the fourth inning for the Redlegs. In a rare moment of wildness, Kerr issued the third baseman "a free pass." Walking a hitter to lead off an inning usually brings trouble to the pitcher. It would not be the case on this occasion. Groh moved to second as Rousch was retired on a grounder to Risberg. Pat Duncan lined to "the Swede" who made a quick toss to Eddie Collins doubling Groh off of second base. A leadoff walk but no harm done.

Groh retired Chick with a fine "scoop and throw" to begin the Sox fourth.[94] The Swede swatted a line drive to right field that eluded Neal, Risberg winding up at third base. Ray Schalk was

---

94    Ibid. Accessed 4 December, 2004.

called upon to execute the often difficult "squeeze bunt." Ideally, the runner races in from third, the hitter gets the bat on the ball for a grounder. The runner scores while the defense attempts to retire the hitter. The play is beautiful when it works. The sequence is really embarrassing if the ball is missed by the hitter or he pops the pitch up resulting in one or possibly two outs. This being the case, a manager will seldom call this play with an unreliable hitter "at the dish." This time the play worked to perfection. Schalk dropped a bunt that hopped over Fisher's outstretched hand.[95] Risberg scored and Cracker was safe at first on the play. Ray was "erased" (as a runner, not as a person) as he was caught trying to steal second on the next play. Kerr grounded out Kopf to Daubert ending the inning.[96] The White Sox had added another run. On this day, three would be more than enough.

Larry Kopf opened the "Reds fifth" with a line drive single past Eddie Collins into right field. It would be Cincinnati's final safety. Neale, Rariden and Fisher grounded weakly to the infield and the small threat was over.

Sherry Magee batted for Fisher in the eighth inning. Dolf Luque, "one of the first Cubans to succeed in the majors,"[97] finished up for Cincinnati.

On this given day, Cincinnati's talented ball club was no match for the guile of one small, courageous left handed pitcher. Kerr had held the Reds to three hits and made three early White Sox runs stand up for a 3-0 win.

The Reds had sent Ray Fisher to the hill to oppose Kerr in the third game of the Series. Fisher was a "poised, studious right hander"[98] who amassed a creditable 100-94 record in his ten year

---

[95]   Ibid. 2. Accessed 4 December 2004

[96]   Ibid. Accessed 4 December 2004

[97]   "Dolf Luque." http://www.baseballlibrary.com/baseballlibrary/ ballplayers/L/Luque_Dolf.stm. Accessed 21 October, 2005.

[98]   "Ray Fisher." http://www/baseballlibrary.com/ballplayers/F/Fisher_Ray. stm. 1. Accessed September 23, 2005.

big league career. A year later as baseball banned the use of the "spitball" Fisher was one of the few who would be allowed to continue to use the serving until the end of his career. Unfortunately, the end of Fisher's career would come "all too soon."

Amazingly, Ray Fisher would be placed on baseball's "permanently ineligible" list shortly after the eight Chicago White Sox had initiated the group. In 1921 Fisher asked the Reds for his "unconditional release" that he might accept a position as baseball coach and assistant football coach at the University of Michigan. Instead, on June 14 of that year the commissioner suspended him for "contract jumping."[99] Fisher would serve at the University of Michigan for thirty eight years. Late in his life, with Landis long dead, the former pitcher was readmitted to the game and tutored pitchers for the Braves and Tigers. Kennesaw Mountain Landis did not ruin Fisher's life. The judge did, however, profoundly affect it. As Victor Luhrs noted "In reviewing this (the Black Sox) and other scandals handled by Judge Landis we find him to be completely and repeatedly inconsistent. He was inclined to show no mercy to the stupid, the alcoholic or the helpless, and then show astonishing lenience toward the smart, well-heeled, the jail worthy."[100] Soon the future of eight ballplayers would rest with such a man. Fate did take strange turns for both teams in this "Fall Classic."

---

[99]   "Ray Fisher." http://www.baseballlibrary.com/baseballlibrary/ballplayers/F/Fisher_Ray.stm. 2. Accessed. September 23,2005.
[100]  Luhrs, Victor. *THE GREAT BASEBALL MYSTERY THE 1919 WORLD SERIES.* A. S. Barnes and Company. New York 1966. 8.

# CHAPTER EIGHT

While Cincinnati still lead the event two games to one it seemed as though Chicago was still competitive to take the World Championship. Much would depend upon the efforts of Edie Cicotte in game four.

Jimmy Ring might well have pitched the best game of his life against Cicotte and the Sox in the next game of this World Series. Ironically, the 1919 episode was not this hurler's first encounter with the attempt to "cook" a baseball game by other players. This was the "same Jimmy Ring" who Hal Chase had attempted to "buy" in a game slightly more than two years earlier. It would not be surprising if such goings on would make the totally honest pitcher a perpetual cynic.

The right handed hurler scattered three hits in a route going performance. Everyone agreed that his effort had been remarkable. Unfortunately, as with all performances within this event, the question will always be: "Was it real?" Jimmy had a serviceable twelve year major league career with the Reds, Phillies, Giants and Cardinals. Ring won one hundred eighteen games while losing one hundred forty nine. The best quality of Jimmy's career was his longevity in the major leagues while toiling for often mediocre teams. As for this particular October day in 1919 we choose to say, "Good job, Jimmy" and hope that it is enough.

"Loyalty" and "professional sports" are not necessarily incompatible terms. When "winning" and "money" are added to the equation in professional baseball, however, relationships become complicated. In spite of his efforts in the 1919 World Series, slightly more than one season later the Reds traded Jimmy Ring. Ring and Greasy Neale were dispatched to the Phillies for left handed pitcher Eppa Rixey.[101] Ironically, Rixey led the National

---

[101] "Jimmy Ring." www.baseballlibrary.com/baseballlibrary/ballplayers/R/ JimmyRing. 2. Accessed 25 September, 2005.

League in losses in 1920 with twenty two. Dick Ferrell was correct; it takes a very good pitcher to lose twenty games in a season. If an incompetent hurler was amassing this many defeats, he would be replaced by someone with more talent. Rixey would eventually be inducted into the Hall of Fame. Still, the Cincinnati Reds would exhibit "short memories" regarding those who had served well in the 1919 World Series, including Jimmy Ring.

"The ballplayers" had not been paid after Kerr's performance. Eliot Asinof notes that the players and the gamblers were beginning to lack trust in each other. Many of those bettors who were unfortunate enough to bet the Series "game by game" were left penniless by Dickie's masterpiece. This game would mark the exit of "Sleepy Bill" Burns and Billy Maharg from the picture.[102] It is ironic that those who initiated the wagering portion of the plot were now destitute. This venture was developing into the all time "tangled web of deception." Those, as Rothstein, who had "bet the entire Series", were still solvent. Sport Sullivan had promised Gandil another payment.[103] We presume that the players expected this money "SOON!" Cicotte was an "early leader in the contest" with his money already received. What Knuckles would do in game four was anybody's guess (or "bet," if you will.)

Anyone who has ever tried to pitch to win a baseball game would have to marvel at Eddie Cicotte's effort in Game Four of this World Series. On Saturday October 4, 1919 it was Eddie's turn to pitch just well enough to lose-barely. Chicago was well matched against Jimmy Ring of the Reds. If the order of rotation means anything, Ring was the National League team's fourth best starting pitcher. This day the hurler did not throw as though this were fact. Ring acted as a "number one starter" for the league champions. He held the mighty White Sox to no runs and only three hits in a nine inning performance.

---

[102] Asinof. *EIGHT MEN OUT.* 99
[103] Ibid. 101

Cicotte, on the other hand, was nearly as brilliant. Cincinnati scratched out only five hits. The first of these came leading off the ballgame. Morrie Rath lined a single over Bucky's head into left. A White Sox fan could have been forgiven for thinking "here we go again." Daubert grounded into a quick: E. Collins to Risberg to Gandil double play.[104] The Chicago fans would be pardoned for thinking that "a bullet had been dodged."

The White Sox did nothing in the initial inning. Nemo popped to Daubert. Cocky did the same to Rath and Weaver lined to Neale in right.

The top of the second was equally uneventful. Big Edd took Cicotte's second pitch to Jackson in left. Joe had no trouble with this one, one down. Pat Duncan popped to Eddie Collins at second. Knuckles caught Larry Kopf looking at a sharp curve for strike three.[105]

Jackson started the bottom of the second with a pop fly double that neither Neale nor Rousch could corral. Happy sacrificed Joe to third, from Ring to Rath covering first. Chick popped a slow curve just in front of the plate. Joe could go nowhere as Groh handled the play easily. The Swede walked and stole second. Schalk walked to fill the bases. Cicotte was up next. Eddie would be no "automatic out" this time. Morrie Rath had to make a beautiful running stop[106] in order to fire to first to retire Cicotte and end the inning.

Neale led off the next inning by grounding to Weaver. Buck made the easy toss to first for out number one. Wingo singled to center but was out stealing moments later. Ring struck out. A quick inning for Cicotte.

The White sox responded with nothing. Leibold lined to Neale to begin the Chicago third. Ring lost control of a curve

104  http://www.blackbetsy.com19game4htm. 1. Accessed 4 December, 2004.
105  Ibid.
106  Ibid.

that plunked Eddie Collins in the ribs. Cocky moved to second as Weaver grounded to Daubert, unassisted. Jackson slapped a first pitch grounder to Rath. Maurice booted this one. Eddie was now at third and Joe holding first. It all came to naught as Felsch grounded to Groh and was retired third to first.

The Reds hit the ball squarely a couple of times in their fourth. The difficulty of hitting a "round ball" with a "round bat' "squarely" has never been lost on followers of the game. Rath lined to Jackson to start the frame. Daubert didn't do so well, bouncing one off of the plate, Schalk threw to Gandil for the second out. Groh lined one sharply but directly into Eddie Collins' grasp.[107]

The Sox' bats were still listless in their half. First Chick grounded out, the Swede flied to Greasy Neale in right, Cracker concluded with an easy fly to Neale in right.[108]

While each team is allotted twenty seven outs in every game, there is usually one inning that is the "turning point. " In this game the inning was the fifth. More specifically, it was the "top" half of that frame. Edd Roush led off the inning with a dribbler in front of the plate and was retired: Schalk to Gandil. Pat Duncan grounded back to the mound. Cicotte fumbled the shot and then threw late to Chick at first. The White Sox first baseman allowed the throw to elude him and Duncan beat Schalk's backup throw to second.[109]

The next play is typical of the confusion that has always made this World Series so interesting. With Pat Duncan on second base Larry Kopf lined a single to left field. Joe Jackson, who had always claimed that he gave maximum effort, fielded the ball cleanly and fired in the direction of the plate attempting to throw out Duncan. Eddie Cicotte "the man with the ten grand" attempted to cut off the throw and bobbled it. One run in and Kopf on

---

[107]  Ibid. 2.
[108]  Ibid.
[109]  "Jimmy Ring." www.baseballlibrary. Accessed 25 September, 2005. 2.

second base. Greasy Neale then doubled over Jackson's head and the Reds had two.[110] It was all that they would need.

Psychologically, the best time to answer a move by the opposition is immediately, before momentum can continue to build. There would be no such answer from the White Sox on this day. Cicotte began the Sox' fifth with an easy grounder to Daubert and was retired easily on the throw to Ring covering. Leibold grounded to Groh who threw past first for a two base error. Nemo was unable to advance as Eddie was retired on a grounder to Groh who fired to Rath covering. Becky bounced to Daubert, unassisted, for the final out of the inning.

Cincinnati hoped, of course to "pad the lead" in the sixth. Eddie Cicotte would permit none of this. Morrie Rath grounded easily to the Swede. Daubert's bounder was hit harder but "easy pickings" for Eddie Collins. He also fired to Gandil for out number two. Groh slapped a fastball to Weaver the third out was "easy." Cicotte was once again in command of the situation. None of the three hitters of the visitors could lift the ball off of the ground.

Jackson could not "pull" a Jimmy Ring offering to start the Sox half of the frame. Larry Kopf threw him out. Happy drove Pat Duncan to the left field wall to pull down a long blast. Gandil lined the White Sox second hit of the game through the visitor's infield. Risberg's long fly to right was handled near the foul line on a slick play by Greasy Neale.[111] Chicago was hitting the ball harder but it counted for nothing in their sixth.

Rousch led off an inning for the third time in the Reds' seventh. It is unusual for this to happen to anyone in the batting order other than the "leadoff man" who, of course, has a third of this task performed as the first inning begins for the team. It could have brought some comfort to the White Sox to see the

---

[110]  http://www.blackbetsy.com/19game4.htm.2..
[111]  Ibid

big man swing with no men on base in every at bat on this day. It may have mattered little; the great slugger had no hits in his three at bats on this day.

Victor Luhrs indicated how different Big Edd was compared to many baseball stars of his era. "Rousch lost all interest in the game when the season ended. He never appeared for spring training, but usually spent that period holding out for a higher salary. When he did appear in uniform, usually right before or right after the opening game, he was in top condition and able to run rings around most players who had sweated out the spring in training camp."[112] If some judged his "love for the game" to be less than comparable stars, his abilities certainly were not.

This turn produced a grounder by Rousch to Cocky Collins. The smooth fielding infielder had no trouble with this one. The toss to Chick produced out number one. Bucky made a great stop behind third and fired a bullet to Gandil barely retiring Pat Duncan.[113] I never saw Buck Weaver play, but his defense is mentioned in the same breath as that of Brooks Robinson and Mike Schmidt. I have marveled at the defensive genius of these players. These men were considered to have been able to "perform magic" with a third baseman's glove. This play is termed "classic Weaver." This third baseman must really have been "something to see" as a defender. Larry Kopf bounded easily to Chick Gandil who retired him unassisted.[114]

It was time for the "seventh inning stretch." This activity would become a baseball tradition. This would be a time for the fans to grab quick refreshments and make "a comfort stop?" It should be noted that in any fair sized crowd the pause is not usually long enough. Many fans may have missed the early portion of the bottom half of the seventh inning.

---

[112]   Luhrs. *THE GREAT BASEBALL MYSTERY: THE 1919 WORLD SERIES.* 34.

[113]   www.blackbetsy.com.19game4htm.2.

[114]   Ibid. Accessed 4 December, 2004

All of those who were absent missed only a little pain inflicted upon Ray Schalk. Jimmy Ring hit Cracker right in the middle of the back with one of his servings. The pitch would prove unpleasant, but not harmful to either Schalk or Ring. Cracker continued in the game. Cicotte would sacrifice the catcher to second. After Rath and Daubert had retired "Knuckles," Chicago could do no further damage. Nemo fouled out to Big Edd Rousch and Cocky grounded out Daubert, unassisted. [115] Jimmy Ring was still, almost single handedly, in control of the ballgame.

It was a good thing for the Reds that they already had enough runs. The eighth inning was "smooth sailing" for Eddie Cicotte and the Chicago White Sox. Neale dribbled "out" Cicotte to Gandil. Ivey Wingo smashed a single. This runner merely set the table for a double play. Ring accounted for two outs from Cicotte to Risberg to Gandil.

Weaver blooped what would later be called a "Texas League" fly ball into short right- center field. Morrie Rath raced out to make a "splendid"[116] catch in between Daubert and Neale who were also in hot pursuit. It was definitely "Jimmy Ring's day." Ring struck out "Shoeless Joe" with a high fastball. Getting this serving past Jackson was akin to trying to "sneak the sunrise past a rooster"- it didn't happen very often. Felsch drove the final hit off Ring over the third base bag. Gandil became another Ring strike out victim. Chick took strike three to end the inning.

The ninth inning was anti climatic. For the Reds: Rath fouled out to Cracker. Jackson made a fine running catch of a Daubert drive. Groh also fouled out to Schalk. It seems as though Cicotte was just as affective at the end of the game as he had been at the beginning.

Risberg began the last of the ninth by grounding back to Ring for out number one. Schalk showed a glimmer of hope for

---

[115]  Ibid. 3. Accessed 4 December, 2004. 3.
[116]  Ibid.

the home team by drawing a walk. Eddie Murphy (no, not that "Eddie Murphy"- this one was an outfielder) was selected to hit for Cicotte. The veteran flied out to Rousch on the first pitch. Nemo Leibold had one more chance. He was retired on a dazzling play from Groh to Jake Daubert. [117] Chicago had not only lost, they hadn't even scored.

Cicotte had pitched almost as well as Ring. Perhaps even more important to "the plan" Eddie had earned another start when his turn came again.

Chick Gandil distributed another twenty thousand dollars of Sport Sullivan's money after the game.[118] The ballplayers were still "used and abused" but also now placated. "The Fix" now more resembled "the Patch Up" but the thing was continuing.

---

[117]   Ibid.

[118]   Asinof, *EIGHT MEN OUT*,103.

# CHAPTER NINE

It rained in Chicago Sunday October 5, 1919. It is not known what all of the consequences of this participation were upon the earth-maybe the rain helped the corn and beans, but the sod of Comiskey Park was to wet to play baseball on. The game was rescheduled for Monday October 6. Lefty was scheduled to be starting for the Sox, Hod Eller for Cincinnati.

It is time to dispel the notion that manager William "Kid" Gleason must have been either stupid or naïve to fail to intercede in the events that were happening around him. During Sunday's rain delay (that was shortly to become "a rain out") a reporter asked Gleason if Williams would be his starting pitcher when the Series resumed. "No," the Kid replied, "I think I'll go myself."[119]

The Kid may have momentarily longed for the baseball of a couple of decades before. In that period a team often had "their pitcher" who would start virtually all of the games for a ball club. It was this environment that allowed those of fantastic talent to set hurling records that will never be rivaled. It would take a starting pitcher twenty five twenty win seasons to come within eleven of Cy Young's record total of five hundred and eleven. It would take a very good pitcher three seasons to equal the single season record of fifty nine wins achieved by Charles "Ole Hoss" Radburn for Providence in 1884. Radburn had accumulated the amazing total of three hundred and nine wins in only *eleven seasons* from 1881 to 1891. This effort must have taken a terrible toll on Radburn's body, as he died a mere six years later at the age of forty two.[120] Times had changed and the Kid had no such athletes available. Being years past his prime Gleason knew that he,

---

[119]  Ibid., 104.
[120]  "Charley Radburn." *THE BASEBALL ENCYCLOPEDIA* Edited by Pete Palmer and Gary Gilette. Barnes and Noble Books. New York. 2004. 1131.

himself, was not an option. The skipper had to "deal from" the active roster at his disposal. Unfortunately, the White Sox were out of aces. For better or worse, Lefty Williams it would be.

In baseball several consecutive zeros on the scoreboard always indicate good pitching. Game five would begin exactly this way. The Reds threatened in the top half of the first. Rath started the game with a walk. Jake Daubert perfectly executed the customary sacrifice bunt to move Maurice to second. Heinie Groh lifted a routine fly to center field. Felsch quickly threw to Risberg, holding Rath at second.[121] The mild threat ended as Rousch grounded out harmlessly.

When a person is a fan of what is considered a "great ball club" there is always hope. The highly touted athletes who "you root for" can always come back from adverse situations. This is how the Chicago backers must have felt as the Sox began the "home half" of the first inning. Nemo Leibold drew a walk to begin the frame. Kopf grabbed Cocky Collins' grounder and fired him out at first. While the Reds were nipping Eddie an argument followed. After initially returning to first, Leibold surprised everyone with a wild dash for second  Nemo looked really good as the Reds could not retire him. The question remains, if Collins had been called safe would the Reds then have been able to force Leibold at the "middle sack"? In the end, it mattered little. Weaver slammed a single off of Eller's glove but Jackson popped to Groh and Felsch flied to Duncan and the White Sox failed to score.[122]

How good was Claude "Lefty" Williams? "What might have been" was demonstrated In the Cincinnati half of the second inning on October 6, 1919. Lefty struck out Pat Duncan. Kopf popped a foul behind the plate. This one was "easy pickings" for Schalk. Cracker was playing his heart out on this day, he always

---

[121]　http://www.blackbetsy.com/19game5.com. 1
[122]　Ibid.

did. Neither the gamblers nor the Black Sox would ever have approached the diminutive catcher about ever giving less than his best effort. It is interesting to note, however, that at least one observer believed that if *only one player* could be bought to throw *only one game* it would be the catcher. According to Luhrs, "He could signal for the wrong pitches, relay pitch signals to the opposing coaches and let bases be stolen against him. As guardian of home plate he could let vital runs across."[123] Had anyone ever accused the heroic Schalk of entertaining any of these thoughts, their next conversation might have been conducted toothless.

Greasy Neale also struck out. Three outs with nary a ball stroked into fair territory. You can't get much better than that!

For the second inning, Hod Eller was his equal. Chick, the Swede and Cracker struck out in succession. Three outs as no one hit the ball at all. This was the poorest of a floundering offensive performance from the White Sox.

Chicago was in the midst of a scoreless streak that would reach twenty six innings. With all of the blame that has been laid at the feet of Cicotte and Williams, the old saying that "you can't win if you don't score" would be proven again. Weaver, Felsch, Jackson, Gandil, Risberg were the heart and soul of the Chicago lineup. Throughout the entire Series they would contribute virtually nothing. McMullin, of course, would receive very little chance. Had they wanted to, Chicago could have outscored the pitching mistakes. They key was that far too few of them wanted to.

Bill Rariden began the third with a soft bounder to Gandil, unassisted. Eller popped one into the "right handed batters box." Bucky took charge, hollered his teammates away and made the

123 Luhrs. *THE GREAT BASEBALL MYSTERY: THE 1919 WORLD SERIES*. 88.

catch easily. Rath was overeager for a Williams' change up and popped to Gandil down the first base line.[124]

Eller ran his consecutive strike out streak to six, getting Williams, Leibold and Eddie Collins in the Chicago half of the inning. Williams never could hit, at least Nemo and Cocky were "trying." Eller was the master of the game thus far. The Chicago fans recognized this effort with a standing ovation for Eller at the conclusion of the frame.[125]

Cincinnati caused a slight stir in there next "at bats." Daubert began the effort harmlessly, "skying" to Felsch in left center. Groh grounded straight to Risberg.[126] Surprise, surprise, the Swede bobbled it. The visitors' third baseman was safe at first. Rousch forced Heinie at second. Rousch stole second. It is difficult to determine if this was a tribute to Edd's speed or the fact that Schalk dropped the pitch. The official scorer gave the benefit of the doubt to the center fielder as Ray was not given an error. This choice mattered little. Pat Duncan flew to Jackson in left ending the top of the fourth. [127]

Eller could have done the bottom of the fourth all by himself. As long as Rariden was present to catch and Daubert was there to touch first base, everyone else could have sat in the dugout. Weaver rolled out Hod to Daubert. Jackson did exactly the same thing. Felsch swung and missed at a wide curve ball for strike three.[128] Not much effort to that one!

Larry Kopf finally registered the Reds' first hit leading off the fifth. "Nothing" followed. Neale tried to sacrifice but was unsuccessful. Kopf was forced from Risberg to E. Collins. A "hit and run play" went wrong when the Sox "pitched out." Rariden missed the serving and Neale was thrown out Ray Schalk to

124   http:/www.blackbetsy.com./ 19game 5.com. 2.
125   Ibid.
126   Ibid.
127   Ibid.
128   Ibid. 2.

Risberg. Bill then flew out to Happy and the threat had been averted.

In the bottom half Cracker singled after Gandil and Risberg had been retired. The inning ended quickly as Eller struck Lefty out on an unusually quick fastball.[129]

After five innings Game 5 was knotted at no score. Both Eller and Williams were at the top of their game. Cincinnati did not achieve their first hit until there were two outs in the fifth inning. No harm came of that drive and after five innings the game was scoreless. Hod Eller led off the sixth inning with a routine fly ball that at least two accounts[130] [131] indicate that either Jackson or Felsch could have handled Neither of the White Sox did. "Hail, Hail, the gang's all here..."[132] Felsch threw badly to Risberg who mishandled the throw. Eller wound up at third. As Chicago moved the infield "in" a few steps closer to the plate, planning to cut off a try for a run with any grounder, Morrie Rath slapped a ground ball past Eddie Collins. Eller scored. Ground balls through "drawn in" infields happen all of the time. This run should have never scored because Eller should have never been on third base at all! Daubert sacrificed, Groh walked, Rousch tripled on a ball that many thought Felsch should have caught.[133] Both Rath and Groh scored. The play at the plate on Heinie was so close that many felt that Cracker had tagged him for the out. Schalk certainly felt that he had made the play. A long, rowdy argument followed. During the altercation the Chicago catcher screamed at, charged and bumped into the home plate umpire. Such contact is expressly forbidden in baseball. Cracker was

---

[129] Ibid.
[130] http://www.blackbetsy.com/19game5.com, 2.
[131] Asinof, *EIGHT MEN OUT*. 105.
[132] "Hail, Hail, The Gangs All Here," available from http://www/miejs. mog/gpv/kids/lyrics/hailhail.htm. 01January, 2005. Words by D. A. Eastron music by Theodore Morse and Arthur Sullivan, 1917. 1.
[133] Asinof, *EIGHT MEN OUT*, 106.

ejected from the proceedings. Byrd Lynn was inserted to catch for the Sox. "As the smoke cleared," the Reds had four runs. Lefty was brilliant the rest of his stint. In further answer to the sportswriter's question, Erskine Mayer finished the game for Williams. Gleason never did have to "toe the rubber" but the Reds were victorious 5-0

# CHAPTER TEN

In the best of circumstances trailing in a "best of nine" series four games to one and returning to the ballpark of the rival would present a daunting task. Chicago was not playing in "the best of circumstances." Fortunately for the Sox, or at least for the members trying for a win. Richard Henry Kerr would make his second start of the Series in Game Six.

Dickie Kerr became a legend in the sixth game of the 1919 World Series. In August of 1919 if someone had told a baseball fan, particularly a White Sox "backer." that Dickie Kerr would be the "ace" of the Chicago staff when (not "if" it was presumed that "the Sox" would make it,) the team made the World Series, most would have laughed. This was the team of Faber, Cicotte and Williams. The small left handed hurler would be unlikely to gain one start in such a Classic. It has been said that "life is funny." By October of 1919 not only was Dickie the "ace" of the South Side of Chicago team, he was the only one of those with the expertise to be a starter whom the ball club could count on for his maximum effort on the hill. Once again, Dickie Kerr would not disappoint.

This author was first introduced to this individual as a radio announcer eulogized, "The man who had won two games as his teammates tried to lose a World Series." While this statement was not totally correct- it is believed that even the "Black Sox" were trying to win both games that Kerr pitched. The motivation of some of the Chicago players may have been wrong: greed, pride, revenge or whatever the results certainly were not. The point of the long ago given quote was well taken. The reporter was defining a hero. Looking back no fault should be found in the statement- it was close enough for folklore.

For all of the "pre Series" discussion of the "great Chicago pitching staff," the Sox used only three different starters during this confrontation. The Reds used five. This diversity of performers on the hill for Cincinnati was either a tribute to the depth of Moran's staff or at least the uniformity of it. As Dutch Ruether opposed Kerr it was the first time Cincinnati had used a repeat starter.

Shano Collins began the game by stretching the count full before popping to Rath in short right-center field. Eddie Collins hit his quite a bit further. Rousch tracked this one down in deep center field. Bucky pounded a single off of Kopf's glove at short for a single. Groh easily handled Shoeless Joe's pop up to third to end the initial "at bats"for the visitors...

The Reds "threatened" in the bottom half of the inning, but they did not score either. After Rath popped to Risberg and Daubert was retired Kerr to Gandil, Groh doubled and Rousch singled off of Risberg's glove at short.  The Swede recovered quickly and fired to third. Risberg's lackluster play overall in the Series has been repeatedly revisited. Plays such as this show that the shortstop, in fact, could wield a pretty good glove- when he wanted to. Groh had rounded the bag too far and couldn't avoid Buck's quick tag. A possible Cincinnati rally had been averted. This wasted effort would later prove critical in a "one run" game. Had the Reds scored, the game might not have gone ten innings and the eventual heroics of Kerr and (amazingly) Weaver, Jackson and Gandil would have never come to pass.

Happy opened the second by connecting with one to the opposite field. Greasy Neale ran it down "within a few yards" of the fence in right.[134] Chick slapped a grounder to Kopf who fired to first for out number two. Risberg flied to Neale, who was- no doubt grateful for all of the early inning exercise, to retire the side.

Risberg bobbled Pat Duncan's easy grounder to begin the

---

[134]  "The 1919 World Series Game 6." available from http://www.black-betsy.com/19game6html. Accessed 4 December, 2004. 1.

bottom half of the frame. Kerr was not often "rattled" by defensive mistakes, but he may have been on this occasion. Dickie followed the error by walking Larry Kopf on four consecutive pitches. If Kerr had not quite regained his composure, Weaver helped him out on the next play. Neale bunted back to the mound. Kerr's throw, attempting the force at third, was wide of the bag. Bucky made a one handed stab and kept his foot on third base to force Duncan.[135] Bill Rariden grounded to Eddie Collins who tossed to Risberg to force Greasy at second. The runners were now at first and third but there were two down. Ruether ended the threat by rolling to Kerr who flipped to first to retire the opposing hurler easily.

Schalk coaxed a walk from Ruether to open the third. Dickie Kerr *knew* how to play the game. A sacrifice was in order and a sacrifice it would be. Groh fielded the roller and fired to Rath covering first. The Chicago hurler was retired but Schalk had moved into scoring position at second with one down. It seemed as though the time was right for a Chicago score. A hit would bring Cracker in and the talented (and honest) Collinses were due at the plate. While the hitting didn't disappoint, the Sox were held scoreless. First Shano hit a high fly that was handled by Rousch in short center. Cocky followed with a line drive to left center of which Pat Duncan made a "beautiful catch."[136]

This game must have been a pleasure to watch. The craftsmanship of Kerr was closely matched by the guile of Leonard. The "Dutchman" lasted into the sixth inning and was responsible for all of the runs Chicago scored. Jimmy Ring pitched more than three scoreless innings to finish up, but it was too late. Kerr was not nearly as affective the second time around against the Reds. The White Sox gave up a pair of runs each in the third and fourth innings.

---

135 Ibid.
136 Luhrs. *THE GREAT BASEBALL MYSTERY; THE 1919 WORLD SERIES.* 289.

In the bottom of the third Daubert singled with one out. Kerr hit Big Edd with a pitch. Years later such activity might have sparked a near riot on the ball field. The home team would start a fight to "protect their star." The visitors would respond behind their pitcher. Hopefully, no one would be hurt in the subsequent donnybrook. It is not ours to say that the participants in the "dead ball era" were more mature, but "close pitches" were considered a part of doing business. Rousch trotted to first base and Kerr prepared to face the next batter. No further incident ensued.

Kerr did pay a price for hitting Rousch. Pat Duncan followed with a triple. The Reds had the first two runs of the game.

After the White Sox were scoreless in the top of the fourth, Cincinnati struck again. Greasy Neale opened with a double and moved on to third as Shano misplayed the ball. Rariden grounded out to Eddie Collins, Neale made no attempt to score. Ruether, a fine hitting pitcher, rapped a double down the left field line and Neale scored easily. Rath grounded to Risberg who hit Ruether in the back with the throw attempting a force at third. Ruether scored and Morrie streaked to second. Rath stole third and it looked as though the White Sox were in for even more trouble. Kerr carefully worked out of the inning. Jackson grabbed Daubert's short fly and fired to the plate where Rath bowled Schalk over trying to dislodge the throw. Cracker held on and tagged the Reds' second baseman out to end the turn at bat but the Reds held a 4-0 lead.

With this early deficit many were considering this World Series "over." The White Sox found some pride left and came back with a run in the top of the fifth. Risberg and Schalk drew consecutive walks to begin the frame. Kerr now contributed with his "stick" grabbing an infield hit. Risberg overran third base on this one (deliberately?) but Groh, perhaps upset by not getting the "out" call reacted slowly after receiving Kopf's throw in a force attempt at third and the Swede scrambled back safely. It looked as though the White Sox might finally be on the verge of a rally of several runs. Chicago fell short of that hope. Shano popped to shallow right field. The drive was so short that Risberg dared not test Rousch's legendary throwing arm and held at third. Eddie Collins did slightly better, driving Big Edd deep enough that Risberg could score. Schalk did not try to advance, unfortunately Kerr did. When the pitcher realized that he was headed for an "occupied base" he stopped between first and second. Groh sprinted across the diamond to tag Dickie for the third out. The inning was over but the White Sox had a run on only one hit.[137]

It was important that Kerr shut the Reds down in the bottom half of the inning that the White Sox might maintain the momentum that they had gained for one of the few times in the Series. Once again, the southpaw got the job done. Groh flew out to Happy. Shano Collins retired Rousch with a nice running catch.[138] Duncan drove a drive to deep center; Felsch misjudged it, caught up to it at the last second and then dropped the ball. It was ruled a double. Kopf was retired Risberg to Gandil.[139] Once again Kerr had performed his "Houdini Act" and the Reds had gone scoreless.

The White Sox added to the fifth inning run with three more in the sixth. Weaver was behind in the count 1-2 when he popped up between Duncan and Kopf. It was one of those plays which either man could make but neither did.[140] The official scorer called the "blooper" a double. Jackson jumped on the first pitch lining a single over second scoring Buck. Felsch doubled to left, scoring Joe and ending Ruether's effort. Once again "the Dutchman" had done a most workmanlike job against one of the finest offensive units in baseball.

---

[137] "1919 World Series Game Six." Available from: http://www.blackbetsy. com/19game6.htm. 2 Accessed 4 December, 2004.

[138] Ibid.

[139] Ibid.

[140] Ibid.

Pat Moran signaled to the bullpen for Jimmy Ring. It should be noted that hurlers who worked both as starters and in relief was a much more common practice in "the dead ball" era than in recent history. A pitcher who can perform both tasks was valuable in 1919. This man is a rarer and more precious commodity in the Twenty First Century. A "Jimmy Ring" would be a prize on any pitching staff of any era. While "trying" to sacrifice, Gandil popped out to Daubert at first. Felsch moved to third as Kopf threw out Risberg. Cracker scored Felsch with a hit off of Groh's glove that eluded both he and Kopf long enough for Happy to cross the plate. [141] Schalk stole second but was stranded there as Kerr's splendid bat work was foiled by a fine stop and throw by Heinie Groh.

The score was now tied and those who bet individual games were suffering from nightmares. These folks were probably also in need of antacid pills when the Reds took their turn. After Neale singled off of Kerr's glove, Rariden blasted one to right. Unfortunately, for the Reds Bill's drive was directly into Shano Collins' glove. As Jimmy Ring struck out, Neale was caught trying to steal second. Dickie had made quick work of the Reds' hitters at a very critical time.

Shano Collins was sent to hit against Ring to start the seventh. Shano blasted a shot up the middle but was retired on a fine play by Kopf. Eddie Collins popped out and Weaver grounded out: Rath to Daubert. [142] Jimmy Ring was once again pitching better than he would ever get credit for.

The beauty of the "dead ball era" was that so many of the games were tightly contested. Every "little play" was important when a hard fought lead could not easily be erased by one "three run homer." The Reds played "dead ball" baseball in the bottom of the seventh. Morrie Rath opened with a single to shallow left,

---

[141]    Ibid.
[142]    Ibid. 2.

just in front of Jackson's outstretched glove. Daubert laid down a perfect sacrifice bunt. One can envision only a few sluggers of the latter part of this century who would be able to consistently perform this task. Groh walked. It is expected that Edd Rousch was the last hitter Dickie Kerr would have enjoyed seeing at this moment. The left handed pitcher was up to the challenge in this circumstance. Rousch slapped into a Risberg to Eddie Collins to Gandil double play. All three performers caught the ball and Kerr was out of trouble.

The Sox seemed to have Jimmy Ring "on the ropes" in their eighth inning. Jackson led off with a base on balls. Felsch didn't wait to see if Ring's wildness continued. Happy flied to Neale in right on the first pitch. Gandil had more patience and also drew a walk. Risberg slashed a low line drive to center field. Jackson was so sure that this would be a hit that he headed for third. Rousch fooled Joe with a fine running catch and doubled the Sox runner off of second with a peg to Rath.[143] It is not known if Chicago sportswriter Hugh Fullerton, who was charting "questionable White Sox plays" on his scorecard,[144] made special note of this play, but he very well could have. Many have contended that this was just "lousy base running." With all of the bad baseball included in these games, it might well have been only that. Who can know for sure? The outcome was a "0" on the scoreboard in the Chicago eighth.

Dickie was still "hangin' in there" for the Sox. The bottom of the eighth would include a little help from his "friends" and a brief scare for the Chicago team. Pat Duncan began the inning for Cincinnati by lifting a foul fly in front of the field boxes in short left field. "Friend" Risberg made a fine running grab just in front of the wall for out number one. Kopf scorched a drive up the middle. Dickie used fine reflexes to grab the ball but his hand

---

[143]  Ibid. 3.

[144]  Asinof. *EIGHT MEN OUT.* 47.

was bruised and numb.[145] Gleason sent Bill James to the bullpen to warm up as the trainer administered to his current pitcher. Once again, Kerr's "heart" was the biggest part of his body. The left handed hurler continued on. Next Rariden bounced a single off of Kerr's glove (ouch! I'll bet that *really hurt.*) Fortunately, Jimmy Ring hit the ball elsewhere. The Reds' pitcher's grounder forced Rariden at second from the Swede to Cocky.

Jimmy Ring started the ninth by fooling Ray Schalk with three straight pitches. One might pause to wonder how great a game might have been played with Ring as a starting pitcher hurling against Kerr and every player on each team giving his best effort. What might have been…

Kerr bounced back to the mound and was retired Ring to Daubert. Nemo Leibold drew a walk but the runner was stranded as Eddie Collins flied out to Rousch.

The greatest tactical advantage to being the home team is "last at bats." The White Sox had not scored in the top half of the ninth inning. Should the Reds do so, the Series would be over and they would be World Champions. This would not be the case. As long as his teammates would "catch the ball" Dickie Kerr would not permit to Sox to lose. In this frame, Chicago caught the ball. Rath grounded out Weaver to Gandil. Daubert lined a short single to center. Groh forced Daubert, from the Swede to E. Collins. Groh attempted to move into scoring position with a steal but Cracker threw him out "by several feet"[146] with Cocky applying the tag at second.

"Extra innings" in a World Series game. Baseball usually doesn't get much better than that. This is when the excitement climaxes. It must have been so for the White Sox as Buck Weaver began the extra frame by lashing a short double that eluded Duncan in left long enough Bucky to reach second with a double.

---

145    "The 1919 World Series Game 6." Available from: http://www.black-betsy.com/19game6htm. 3. Accessed 4 December, 2004.

146    Ibid.

Jackson's attempted bunt bounced high in the air and he was credited with a single as Weaver reached third. Chick singled to center (of such things are good statistics made) scoring Weaver and moving Shoeless Joe to second. Schalk's bounder to Kopf would end the rally.

Chicago would score just that single run in the tenth. This would be enough. The Reds would go "three up and three down in their half to end the game. Rousch grounded out to Eddie Collins, second to first. Duncan fouled out to Cracker behind the plate and Cocky made a smooth fielding play and throw to Gandil to retire Kopf.[147]

Kerr, after a rather inglorious start would eventually settle down and go all ten innings. One can only wonder at Dickie's reply had he been asked by Gleason if he could continue for the entire game. I can imagine that it would have been something to the affect of "Are you kidding? If not me, then who? Is there someone else we could trust with the outcome in a game this close?" In any case Kerr was "the man" in a 5-4 victory.

---

[147]   Ibid.

# CHAPTER ELEVEN

Most individuals who "bet" on major league baseball games and most specifically the ones who specialized in wagering on each separate contest were in for "a deep letdown" on October 8, 1919. Logic would have dictated that the 1919 World Series would end with the Game Seven that was played on that date. Eddie Cicotte was starting for the Sox. Cicotte was both "in" and "paid for," right? Wrong! In a strange twist Cicotte pitched a masterpiece. Eddie proved exactly how "out of control the train had become." None of the players ever expected to have their antics discovered. Such trickery had gone unnoticed before. In some cases in which "fixing" had occurred the penalties had not been "fatal."

Cicotte was expecting that he would continue pitching for as many more seasons as his health and talent dictated. Eddie wanted a win in the World Series as an extra "bargaining chip" for his 1920 contract negotiations. While his previous many great seasons had benefited him little, Knuckles knew that a World Series win in October of 1919 would be a tool to use to add money for the next season. This might have been one of the few cards that the aging hurler had to play. Once again it should be noted that it never occurred to the Black Sox that they would be discovered. The Chicago players may well have been "hedging their bets" against non payment from the gamblers. The winners' share of the World Series money would give them a little something, anyway. Chicago and Cicotte never left doubt as to the outcome of Game Seven.

Only 13,923 fans paid their way into Redlands Field a surprisingly small crowd to "root on" their National League Champions for what everyone knew would be the last baseball game in Cincinnati for the season. If The Reds won this one, the season would be over and they would be World Champions. If the White Sox were victorious, Game Eight and if necessary Nine would be hosted by the White Sox back in "the Windy City" at Comiskey Park. So, what happened to all of the people?

Eliot Asinof attributed the poor attendance to a number of reasons. The most absurd was that Reds' hurler Dutch Ruether had been "out on the town" the night before. Be that as it may, Dutch had pitched the day before and was an unlikely participant in this game. As a credit to Ruether's ability, it is believed that he had pitched "hung over" and "well" simultaneously before. Dutch was used only as a pinch hitter and it is doubtful that this appearance was a factor in the game.

The rumors of "fix" could have played a part as well. The questionable plays of the Chicago entry were widely known. The misplay by Kopf and Duncan the day before was also mentioned. Still the "Kopf, Duncan" matters made no sense- who was fixing what? Did Cincinnati owner want a longer match up to increase his own revenue? In the overall economics of the game, one or two more games "on the road" would not have contributed to the Reds income in such a way as to make playing "badly" worth the effort. Asinof also notes that the most logical reason that the people stayed home was the enormous traffic jam surrounding Redlands Field the day before. Perhaps the "city" should have planned better for such an important civic event. Maybe the Reds should have hired additional staffing to direct traffic, park cars and otherwise facilitate fan access to their moment on "center stage" of the baseball performance. The real losers in the "traffic fiasco" were those who faithfully followed the efforts of "their Reds." Only the most loyal supporter of the home team would venture into such congestion two days in a row.[148] Apparently "frustration won out" and the people stayed home.

The fans who did venture forth were best served if they appeared at the ballpark on time. Those who arrived late would miss the "first blood" of the game. The White Sox scored in the

---

[148]  Asinof. *EIGHT MEN OUT.* 110-111.

initial "at bat" of the contest. Shano Collins singled to center field on the third pitch of the game. Eddie Collins grounded to the mound. As Slim Sallee flipped to Daubert to retire him, Shano moved to second. The Chicago right fielder had to hold as Weaver flew out to Edd Roush in center. Jackson singled to left, driving in the first run of the game. Joe moved to second as Felsch bunted for a hit. The first turn of Chicago ended as Gandil forced Happy as Kopf fielded his grounder and flipped to Rath for the put out.

If the "Black Sox" had started brilliantly, their "White Sox" teammates were not doing quite as well. Morrie Rath started for Cincinnati with a routine ground ball to Eddie Collins. The "great one" let it go between his legs for an error. Even future Hall of Fame players are not perfect. Any kid who has ever "dropped one" in a pickup game on the sandlot grew a little closer to Cocky on that one. Daubert swung at the first pitch and popped to Eddie Collins. Groh struck out. Roush forced Daubert. His sharp ground ball was fielded by Cocky Collins who flipped to Risberg for the out. E. Collins' rare miscue did no harm at all.

The second inning was uneventful for both sides Risberg grounded out Kopf to Daubert to start the Chicago half of the frame. Schalk jumped on the first pitch but managed only a short fly to Neale in right. Cicotte fanned and the White Sox were scoreless in their second.

After Duncan was retired to start the Cincinnati half of the frame, Larry Kopf reached on a scratch single. Greasy Neale popped, foul, to Weaver. Kopf tried to steal his way into scoring position, but Ray Schalk was having none of it. Cracker "gunned" a throw to Risberg and Larry's effort at theft was thwarted. Cicotte had silenced the home team in their half of the inning.

The Sox "did some damage" against Sallee in the top of the third. Shano bounced a single up the middle, off of Sallee's glove into center field. Larry Kopf grabbed Eddie Collins' grounder at deep short but could not get either runner. Weaver grounded to short. Larry forced Eddie Collins at second unassisted. When Buck could not be doubled up, the Reds claimed interference by Eddie at second base. After an extended argument Weaver was ruled "out" due to obstruction by E. Collins at second base. Shano had moved to third base, but now there were two outs. Shoeless Joe picked up his teammates with a line single to right scoring S. Collins. Further damage was averted as Felsch grounded to Kopf who tossed to Rath, forcing Jackson at second.[149]

This second run would really be all that Eddie Cicotte would need. Those scored later would be mere "insurance." When "Knuckles" was at his best he never needed many runs.

The Reds could respond with nothing in the bottom of the inning. Wingo led off with a walk but could not advance as Felsch roamed into short right-center field to handle Slim Sallee's pop fly. The "range" of the center fielder is often credited for cutting off possible hits that neither the slower Jackson who patrolled left field nor the Leibold/ Shano Collins tandem in right field could gather in. Happy played center field with vigor! Rath grounded to Risberg. The Swede's toss to Eddie Collins forced Wingo at second. Daubert drilled a "rope" on the ground, but directly at Cicotte. Knuckles made a nice grab and fired to Gandil to get Jake and retire the Reds.

Sallee was more effective in the fourth. Gandil looped a short fly to Neale in right field. Daubert handled Risberg's pop foul between first and the dugout. Schalk pulled a pitch headed for left field. Groh made the stop but could not recover in time to retire Cracker at first. Once again Schalk had used his speed to best advantage. A catcher who runs well is a rarity. The use of the leg muscles to squat behind the plate repeatedly for lengthy periods of time is said to inhibit their usefulness for running speed. The modern training methods of future generations have not

---

[149] "1919 World Series Game 7." available from: http://www.blackbetsy. com/19game7.htm. Accessed 4 December, 2004. 2.

seemed to be able to overcome this anatomical contradiction. A "good running catcher" is still a rarity in baseball today. Schalk may have been the only one of his generation.

In the "Black Sox generation" pitchers were expected to contribute with the bat as well. The ninth bat in the lineup was necessary. All other things being equal (which they seldom were) a pitcher who could hit would be chosen before one who could not. By the 1970s the American League would solve the problem with the "Designated Hitter." The National League did not join in this venture, creating a contradiction that was especially profound when the leagues competed (All Star Games, World Series, and Interleague Play.) In 1919 such compromises would have been considered ridiculous. In this particular case, Cicotte performed well, but unsuccessfully in the "batter's box." Eddie drove the second pitch into deep center field. Rousch used his "Hall of Fame" defensive skills to track the drive down in deep center field. The Sox were scoreless in the fourth.

Knuckles intended to give Cincinnati "no chance." The Reds could not hit the ball out of the infield in the bottom of the inning. First Groh and then Rousch grounded out from Eddie Collins to Gandil. Duncan grounded weakly to Weaver, another throw to Chick and Cicotte could return to the dugout and sit down.

The Sox put Game Seven away in the fifth inning. After Shano Collins flied out to Neale in right, namesake Eddie singled to center field. Bucky sizzled a grounder to Groh. The third baseman bobbled the ball, recovered in time to throw but fired high, pulling Daubert off of the bag. One or the other of the misplays was scored an "error" on Heinie and Weaver was safe at first. Jackson slapped a grounder to Rath at second. If a baseball could have "double play" written all over it, this was the one. Unfortunately for Morrie, he allowed the ball to bounce off of his ankle. The second error of the inning loaded the bases. If great teams are often marked by outstanding defense, lesser squads are often cursed by mediocre glove work. On this day the Reds committed four errors.

Felsch singled to score Eddie Collins and Weaver. Slim Sallee was done for the day and Ray Fisher was in the game. The new pitcher used his glove on the first play. Gandil was retired pitcher to first base. Jackson and Felsch both moved up a base but were stranded as the Swede struck out.[150]

Major league rules require that a starting pitcher must complete five innings to earn a victory in any given game. On this October date in 1919 Eddie Cicotte "blew by" this requirement with ease. In the bottom of the Cincinnati fifth Kopf popped out to Jackson in short left field. The "bug on the windshield" was Greasy Neale who singled to left field. The pressure started to build when Wingo walked. Fisher was due to hit, but a pinch hitter was in order. Cincinnati sent another pitcher, Dutch Ruether to the plate. While Dutch was a good hitter, it was obvious that Moran was hoping to save his better batsmen for a possible rally later. The strategy for this inning was not successful. First, Ruether fouled one off weakly and then rolled a broken bat grounder to end the inning.

The Reds brought Dolf Luque in to pitch in the sixth. The "Pride of Havana" would have little impact on this particular World Series. Adolfo would, however, have a credible twenty year major league career. His presence in this game does give one cause to consider the injustice of the sport in the first half of the Twentieth Century. Non citizens of the United States were always welcome. Luque as a Cuban, "Caucasian" created no stir in the game. Had Dolf had dark skin, he would have never been permitted. Additionally, black citizens of our own country would not be allowed in the major leagues for an additional twenty eight years. It was not until 1947 that Jackie Robinson was allowed to be the first of "his race" to play in the major leagues. This author prefers

---

[150]  Ibid. 2.

to consider Jackie and many other courageous black athletes of his era to be a credit to their race- *the human race.* How could a country as great as this one ever have been so blind? Color blind would have definitely been better. At any rate, Dolf Luque was in to pitch for the Reds.[151]

Cracker began the turn by lifting a fly to Duncan in medium left field. Cicotte fanned. Just as Dolf appeared to be breezing through the inning, Shano Collins ripped a double. The Reds fans smiled, gasped and breathed again as Cocky struck out, the last pitch eluded Wingo and the catcher threw to first to retire the hitter and end the inning.

Eddie Cicotte at his best was brilliant but not perfect. Cincinnati scored in the bottom of the sixth. The frame started out harmlessly enough as Jake Daubert was called out on strikes. Heinie Groh drove one over the temporary left field fence (constructed to retain the overflow of fans in that section.) Under the "ground rules" established for this modification the third baseman was limited to a double. The usually spectacular Rousch was not up to the task on this occasion. Big Edd tapped weakly to Cicotte. While Eddie threw to Gandil to retire Edd, Groh advanced to third. Duncan fired a single to center field scoring Heinie with the first Cincinnati run. The rally ended when Kopf grounded to Eddie Collins. Cocky flipped to Risberg for the easy force of Duncan at second base. This was another circumstance in which Collins and Risberg, who hated each other so, performed flawlessly together on the field. It has been contended that Cicotte could have prevented this run by going to third base to retire Groh on Rousch's routine grounder.[152] Those who allege that this was a misplay are forgetting two things: this choice is often made by a player protecting a four run lead in an effort to prevent more base runners and a possible "big rally" and Cicotte

---

[151]   Ibid. 2.
[152]   Ibid.

was *trying to win this one.* Under these circumstances, it would seem that Knuckles was playing "sound baseball." This should be considered a "rare treat" during this sequence of contests.

By the seventh inning the White Sox were "in control" and perhaps becoming bored. In the top half Weaver struck out, Jackson grounded to Rath and Happy also struck out. Not "White Sox baseball" at its best!

In the bottom portion Eddie pitched just well enough to get by. Greasy Neale struck out. Wingo walked. Luque (why was he still hitting in the last of the seventh with his team behind by three runs?) struck out. Was Moran saving his bench for an eight game that Cincinnati might never need? Was Dolf a better hitter than any of Cincinnati's remaining reserves. Whatever the motivation a "strike out" contributed nothing to the fading cause of the Reds on this particular day. Rath singled to center moving the Reds' catcher to second. Cocky knocked down Daubert's smash and then threw to first to retire Jake "on a close decision."[153] Cicotte had retired "every other hitter." It was enough. Cincinnati had gone scoreless.

As Chicago hit again Chick produced nothing to add to his contract for the next season. The pop fly that he generated was handled by Cincy shortstop Larry Kopf in short left center field. Rousch dropped Risberg's fly in short left field. The promise of a base runner was snuffed out as the Swede tried to stretch the play into two bases. Big Edd recovered in time to throw Risberg out at second base.[154] Kopf made a great stop and threw out Schalk to end the inning.[155]

Heinie Groh's "claim to fame" in the Reds' eighth was that he hit the ball out of the infield. Jackson hauled in his fly in left. Rousch grounded out to Eddie Collins. Duncan did the same to Risberg.

---

[153] Ibid. 3.
[154] Ibid.
[155] Ibid.

Cicotte, apparently concentrating on his hurling task, fanned to start the ninth. Shano lined out to Rousch in center. Eddie Collins grounded out, Daubert unassisted. It was "time to play defense."

The Reds hit the ball well in their last "at bats" but produced no runs. Kopf lined to Eddie Collins. Greasy Neale stroked a routine fly to Jackson in left. Two "last hopes" Wingo and Sherry Magee batting for Luque both singled. Jimmy Smith got his name in the box score running of Magee. His speed made little difference as Rousch lined to Felsch ending the game.

This game should give one pause to consider the superiority of the 1919 Chicago White Sox to their National League opponent. The standings will determine a superior team over an entire season. There are so many games that the "best" team should win the majority of them. With so many magnificent athletes it is almost impossible to anticipate who would win any single game. Despite their failure in the 1919 World Series, the Chicago White Sox won every game that they intended to. That the Sox fans were not rewarded with a World Championship was a tragedy. This is what "the fix" was all about.

# CHAPTER TWELVE

Game eight of the World Series was over before it began. The night before to be exact. Sport Sullivan had been acting on behalf of Arnold Rothstein who had put up the money to "buy" the Chicago players.[156] Game Seven had made AR nervous. Not trusting the White Sox players (I wonder why-tea) "The Big Bankroll" had bet much money on Cincinnati to win the entire Series.[157] He believed that the players could not be trusted on a game by game basis. Rothstein had been proven correct. Arnold made it clear to Sport that the World Series would end with game eight. Sullivan understood the negative consequences of any other outcome not only for the ballplayers but for Sullivan himself. Sullivan's conviction that "the fix" would work had been instrumental in convincing AR to invest in the plan. Mr. Rothstein was not someone that took disappointment well.

The exact nature of the discovery of Mr. Sullivan's actions and that of his employee is unknown- still, the story has been retold so often and in such identical detail that it is hard to disbelieve. It certainly makes sense in the light of Claude Williams' pitching performance in Game Eight of the 1919 World Series. In a scenario worthy of Jimmy Cagney, Sullivan made a telephone call to an associate. An arrangement was made for a partnership in one venture. The Chicagoan was to contact a Mr. Williams and explain that his safety, along with that of his wife would depend upon a poor pitching performance on October 9, 1919.[158] "It wasn't a question of money any more." Williams was not to be paid another dime. He was to lose that ball game or something

---

[156] "The Black Sox" available at http://www.chicagohs.org/history/blacksox/blk4a.html accessed 112904.

[157] Aisnof *EIGHT MEN OUT*, 113.

[158] Ibid. 114.

was going to happen to him. Maybe something might happen to his wife, too."[159]

At this point Lefty was in over his head. He must have realized that the ballplayers were amateurs at playing a game in which "murder for money" was not that unusual. Williams, no doubt, had as much physical courage as the rest of us. The fear for his own welfare must have been dwarfed by the concern for the safety of the woman he would love for his entire adult life. Claude responded as almost any husband would. Money was no longer an issue. The left hander would react in a manner that Illinois community property laws might have deemed "self preservation." He would lose a ballgame. The result of Game 8 was a forgone conclusion.

Claude Williams must have seen little reason to keep the gamblers in suspense. Morrie Rath led off Cincinnati's offensive game with a pop up to Risberg at short. It surely would have ruined everyone's plans if all of the Reds had hit that way and Lefty had pitched a perfect game. Only in my dreams. Jake Daubert lined softly in front of Liebold in center field. The Sox had switched positions for Felsch and Nemo after becoming disgusted with Hap's play in center over the previous games in the Series. Could Hap have caught this ball? How would Felsch have handled the ball if he had fielded it? The questions of this World Series just go on and on. Heinie Groh singled to right. Williams had been throwing only fastballs.[160] Almost all hitters who had gotten to the major leagues had done so by hitting fastballs. When the batter knew what was coming, the hurler had little chance. Big Edd Roush measured another fastball for a standup double to right field. Daubert scored on this drive and Groh moved to third. Pat

---

[159]   Ibid. 117.
[160]   Ibid, 118.

Duncan singled to left scoring two more runs. Gleason had seen enough and called in Bill James.[161]

James probably was not quite ready for such an early entrance. He managed only one strike before walking Larry Kopf. "Big Bill" then settled down enough to fan Neale. Just when it seemed that the agony might be over, Bill Rariden slapped a single to right. Duncan scored on the play and Kopf moved to third. Eller flied to Felsch. "It" had finally ended. As the White Sox escaped to the dugout, they already trailed 4-0.[162]

Chicago could not mount a response in their first. Leibold singled to left and Eddie Collins followed with a "little bingle" to center. The promising start "died on the vine." Eller fanned Weaver. Kopf made an outstanding play gathering in Jackson's foul in front of the left field fence. Felsch went down easily, "fanning"on strikes and ending the inning. No runs in the bottom of the first.

Two out rallies have been known to drive managers nearly insane. One pitch or one stroke of the bat can make so much difference in these circumstances. Bill James must have sent Kid Gleason searching for the antacid pills in the top of the second. The count "went full" to Rath before Morrie struck out. Daubert lined hard to Jackson in left for the second out.[163] William Henry James must have been thinking "so far, so good." They say that all good things must come to an end…Heinie Groh beat out a slow grounder to the right side of the infield. Big Edd Rousch drove a double over Jackson's head and Groh scored. Big Edd's good things also ended as he was caught trying to stretch a double into a triple. This portion of the play went from Leibold (backing up

---

[161] *1919 WORLD SERIES* available from http:www.blackbetsy. com/19game8.htm, 1.

[162] Ibid.

[163] Ibid.

Jackson) to Risberg to Schalk to Weaver to Eddie Collins. At least most of the Chicago team got some exercise.[164]

It is interesting to note the lack of desperation in Kid Gleason's moves in the bottom of the second. After Gandil grounded out to Daubert, unassisted, the Swede walked. Schalk singled to left and Risberg moved to second. At this point, Bill James was allowed to hit for himself. It would seem that a pinch hitter, perhaps Shano or Harvey McClellan might have had a better chance to continue the effort. James would have been done for the day, but "saving" pitching for "tomorrow" would seem to be fruitless at this point.

In defense of the Gleason move, he could well have felt that his team could overcome a four run disadvantage (the Sox did score five.) What the Kid didn't know was if he had any additional hurlers who could shut down the Reds (Cincinnati would get ten.) The Chicago White Sox lost, who knows…

James was assigned to hit for himself and fouled to Groh in front of the Chicago dugout. Hope was still present but it was not Leibold's day to turn things around for his team. Nemo struck out and the chance had passed.

James' job at this point was to "keep the Sox" in the game. Further damage would have almost certainly been fatal to the Chicago cause. Bill hung in there in the third. First he induced Duncan to ground to Weaver. Larry Kopf hit the ball harder, but unfortunately for him, in the same direction. Weaver also threw him out. Greasy Neale walked. Apparently the Reds had not become convinced of the ability of Ray Schalk's throwing arm. They should have been! Neale tried to steal second base and was retired from Cracker to Cocky covering the bag.

Chicago finally broke through against Eller in their third. After Eddie Collins lined to Duncan, Weaver stroked one to short right center and was retired on a fine catch by Morrie Rath.

---

[164]   Ibid. 2.

Jackson followed with a home run into the right field bleachers. The White Sox had a run back. Baseball is a "game of inches" if Buck's drive had fallen, the Sox could have had two. "If wishes were horses, beggars would ride..." [165] The inning ended a moment later as Kopf handled Felsch's grounder and threw him out.

The "game" Mr. James was "staggered" in the fourth, but he did not fall. Chick grabbed Bill Rarien's line drive at first base for the initial out. Hod Eller was hit by a James serving. It is a good bet that James cursed his own mistake. The Cincinnati pitcher should have been forced to "earn" his way onto the bases. Rath stroked a "dribbler" between the mound and second and was credited with a hit as Risberg could not make a one handed stop.[166] Daubert lined a hard single to center. Leibold made a great throw to the plate to retire Eller.[167] Rath moved to third and Daubert to second on this play but it made little difference as Groh popped to Eddie Collins stranding both.[168]

Any thoughts that Hod Eller had started to weaken in the previous inning were quickly dispelled in the fourth. Gandil flied to Neale in right center. The Swede struck out swinging and Schalk grounded out from Groh to Daubert. "'Excellent', I cried. 'Elementary' said he."[169]

Big Edd Rousch hit the first pitch in the fifth hard, but right at Eddie Collins. Cocky fired to Chick for out number one.

[165]  James Hallwell. "If wishes were horses, beggars would ride." Available from Http://www.painterskeys.com/getquotes.asp?fname+cf&ID=74. 4. Accessed 24 December, 2005.

[166]  "1919 World Series: Game 8." www.blackbetsy.com. 2. Accessed 4 December, 2004.

[167]  Ibid. Accessed 24 December 2005.

[168]  Ibid.

[169]  Arthur Conan Doyle. *MEMOIRS OF SHERLOCK* HOLMES. *"The Crooked Man."* Doubleday. 1893. 413. Available from http://members. aol.com_lit_a/shbest/quote/Tqhm.htm. 2. Accessed 12 December, 2005/

Duncan's ball was not quite as hard to handle and Eddie Collins also threw him out. Larry Kopf, batting left handed, pulled a drive into the right field corner and stretched it into a triple as the Sox were retrieving and relaying the ball. Kopf scored as Neale drove one past Risberg into left center. It looked as though there was even more trouble on the horizon as Greasy stole second base. Big Bill gathered himself and avoided further trouble as he induced Bill Rariden to ground out to short.[170]

Again in the bottom of the fifth the opportunity would have seemed right to use a pinch hitter for the pitcher. The Sox desperately needed base runners and Bill James was nearing the end of a typical days work for him during the 1919 season. Again the hurler hit for himself, he fanned. Kopf made consecutive beautiful plays at shortstop retiring first Nemo Leibold and then Eddie Collins with strong throws to first.[171]

The proof that Bill James was, indeed, "cooked" for the afternoon of Thursday October 9, 1919 was immediately apparent as Cincinnati hit in their sixth. Hod Eller took a ball and a strike and then drove a hot single up the middle. What a different game it might have been had Bill James hit as well for Chicago on this day as Eller did for the Reds. Morrie Rath walked and Kid Gleason had seen enough of James for this day. As the big right hander left the mound, the White Sox skipper might well have murmured something about a "job well done." The plight of the home team on this day certainly wasn't caused by relief pitching.

Roy Wilkinson was not immediately able to "stop the bleeding" in this inning. Daubert greeted the new hurler with a bunt in front of the plate. Schalk tried to get Eller at third, but threw badly.[172] None of the runners were retired and the bases were

---

[170]   "1919 World Series: Game 8." available from www.blackbetsy.com. 2.
        Accessed 24 January, 2006.
[171]   Ibid.
[172]   Ibid.

now loaded. Wilkinson retired Groh on strikes but Rousch bounced a single over Eddie Collins' head scoring both Hod and Morrie. The Cincinnati center fielder was just too good a hitter for Chicago to expect to continue to retire him in the tough situations. To make matters worse Jake moved up to third base and Big Edd to second on an ill advised effort to retire Rath at the plate. Daubert did not linger at the hot corner for long. Duncan singled to center allowing him to score. Kopf walked reloading the bases. Neale grounded to Weaver who fired to Cracker forcing Rousch at the plate. Kopf, who had moved to second on the Neale play, was picked off second from Schalk to the Swede. The inning had finally, mercifully ended but the Reds had tacked on three more runs.

The Chicago fans would have been forgiven if they headed for the exits at this point. To their credit, few did. Asinof put it best, "…those 33,000 stalwarts never lost heart. They stuck with them inning after inning, roaring with every Chicago base hit…"[173]

The Chicago efforts to "return service" in the bottom of the sixth while not "feeble" were fruitless. Weaver slashed a grounder past Daubert for a single to right. Joe Jackson flied "deep" to Rousch in center. Big Edd caught up with one by Hap as well. Chick flied to Neale in right. Worthwhile efforts, adding up to nothing.

At least there was no "insult to injury" in the seventh. Bill Rariden flied to Oscar Felsch in center. For one of the few remaining times in his life Happy could feel the joy of wrapping his baseball glove around a tightly stitched baseball in the middle of the grassy pasture of a baseball diamond. It is doubtful that Felsch had either the time or the foresight to properly enjoy the moment.

Wilkinson was certainly skilled enough to whiff the opposing

---

[173]  Asinof. *EIGHT MEN OUT.* 119.

hurler. After he had dealt with Eller, Roy "lost his radar." Rath walked and immediately stole second base. The stolen base was of little consequence. Daubert also took "four wide ones" and was awarded first. Morrie would have been awarded second base even had he not got his uniform dirty with the slide at second base on the previous play. Heimie Groh flied "routinely" (if there can be such a term for a two legged creature chasing a small spiraling object through a breeze several hundred feet from its point of origin) to Nemo Leibold in right field.[174]

The Swede led off the bottom of the seventh and for a moment it looked as though he might have a hit. Rath foreclosed that possibility with a fine running catch in short center field.[175] "Momentum" is a wonderful concept within a sporting contest. It appeared as though the Reds were riding that "wave" to reach heights and make plays that were normally beyond their capabilities.

No further heroics of this nature were required by the Cincinnati defense this particular inning. Cracker popped to Rariden just behind the plate and Wilkinson struck out.[176]

The Reds added yet another run in their eighth. Big Edd Rousch was hit by a pitch to begin the frame. It must have been obvious that Cincinnati was not yet comfortable with their lead. Pat Duncan sacrificed the base runner to second. In later generations this might have been considered "piling on" to an already lopsided score. In this case it could be that Pat Moran and the National League team were still not comfortable with the edge they held on the formidable White Sox squad. Such a maneuver can only be considered a compliment to the prowess of the Reds opponent during this particular confrontation. The move produced no immediate dividends. Larry Kopf fouled to Buck and the runner was unable to advance. Greasy Neale drew

---

174    Ibid. 3. Accessed January, 2006.
175    Ibid.
176    Ibid.

a walk to keep things going and Pat Rariden showed the wisdom of Moran's move with a single to left, scoring Rousch. Risberg threw out Eller and the Reds were, at last, done scoring.

The Chicago White Sox showed a final sign of what they were (had been) made of in the bottom of the eighth inning. After Leibold led off by flying out to Neale in right, Eddie Collins singled to center. Bucky followed with a double to right field. Jackson also doubled to right, scoring both E. Collins and Weaver. Happy popped to Daubert for the second out. Neale lost Gandil's ball in the sun in right and it was scored as a triple.[177] Jackson scored the third run of the inning on the play. Next, Rousch dropped Risberg's short fly in center field (momentarily Cincinnati was playing more as the Black Sox had than repeating their previous performances during this set of games) and Chick scored run number four. The brief Chicago flurry ended as Rath threw out Ray Schalk.[178]

The baseball confrontation that had begun with such fanfare would end with barely a whimper. The Reds got a hit in their half of the ninth as Rath beat out a roller to Risberg. Conventional to the end, the Reds sacrificed. Daubert moved Morrie up with a bunt and was retired from Wilkinson to Gandil. It took only moments for the top half of the inning to end as Groh flied to Leibold and Rousch grounded out from Weaver to Gandil at first.

Eddie Murphy was the pinch hitter for Roy Wilkinson leading off the bottom of the ninth inning. The outfielder "took one for the team" and was awarded first base when he was hit by a pitched ball. Rousch robbed Leibold of a possible double (and the Sox of a potential rally) with a "fine diving catch" in center field.[179] Cocky followed with a single (which might have meant two runs had Nemo's drive fallen) but Leibold could only move to second on the hit. Weaver flied deep enough to Neale that Leibold could move

---

[177]   Ibid. 4. Accessed 28 January, 2006.
[178]   Ibid.
[179]   Ibid.

to third base after the catch. Cocky stole second and Chicago had two runners in scoring position. It all came to nothing. Jackson grounded to Rath who threw him out and the chaos had finally ended. There was no longer anything that humankind could do to manipulate the events of the 1919 World Series.

# CHAPTER THIRTEEN

It would be over thirty years before major league baseball teams had pitchers specializing in "relief." In 1919 hurlers who did not start games were those who were not good enough to do so. Bill James and Roy Wilkinson were not starters. Their efforts, however, made little difference on Thursday October 9, 1919; James gave up three runs and Wilkinson four. During the entire Series no Chicago relief pitcher had made an appearance and held the Reds scoreless.[180] The game was lost by the three that Williams surrendered in the first inning. The White Sox answered only with a run in the bottom of the third inning and four after the game was "out of hand" in the eighth. The final score stood 10-5 against Chicago. As unlikely as it seemed only a few weeks before, the Cincinnati Reds were baseball's World Champions. The 1919 World Series had ended.

John Greenleaf Whittier has written, "Of all sad words of tongue and pen the saddest are these: 'It might have been.'"[181] What might have been…will always surround the 1919 World Series.

William "Kid" Gleason was a hero of this Fall Classic. A "good and honest man" who was also a fine baseball man, Gleason did the very best he could with a team only "half trying" to win the confrontation. It would have been nearly impossible to turn the tide of events that transpired during this particular October. In hindsight however, knowing that Chicago lost the World Series anyway, one cannot help but wonder what would have happened if Gleason had decided to bench those he felt were not performing at their best after the sixth game.

---

[180]   Luhrs. *THE GREAT BASEBALL MYSTERY: THE 1919 WORLD SERIES. 77.*

[181]   "John Greenleaf Whittier." Available from: http://www.barteby. com/100/439.5html. 1. Accessed 4 December, 2005.

Gleason would have pulled Chick Gandil, Swede Risberg, Joe Jackson and Happy Felsch from the lineup. This patchwork effort would now possibly have included: back-up catcher Byrd Lynn at first base. Harvey McClellan would take over at short-stop for Risberg. Bucky would, no doubt, stay at third- for all his "hanging with bad company" Weaver was playing at his best. Eddie Murphy, Leibold and Shano Collins would comprise the outfield. Schalk would continue behind the plate and Eddie Collins at second base. While this lineup might not have been "awesome" it did include five players with extensive experience starting for this pennant winning club. It seems entirely possible that these men could have scratched out enough runs to win Game Eight.

Gleason had already expressed his disgust with the efforts of Claude Williams. The Sox had no one else ready who could go nine innings. A clairvoyant Gleason might have started Bill James and just told him to "go as long as you can." Had James pitched four innings and given up two runs, as he did in Game Eight, Chicago would still have been in the ballgame. Grover Lowdermilk might have been next and then Wilkinson. If the pitching had kept the game closer, perhaps the revamped lineup could have come through earlier in the game. Had the Sox won game eight, who knows what might have happened with Kerr ready to hurl in game nine. This is all conjecture but, as mentioned, this author is a Black Sox fan. Would there have been any investigation at all had the Chicago White Sox won?

We have seen that baseball was not unfamiliar with internal investigations regarding gambling before October of 1919. It is possible that Charles Comiskey could have prevented the deci-mation of his team by pursuing internal remedies. It has been noted, particularly by Victor Luhrs,[182] that, ""Normal proce-

---

[182]    *THE GREAT BASEBALL MYSTERY: THE 1919 WORLD SERIES.*
         *160-161*

dure during the regime of the National Committee would have followed along the lines of these: Comiskey would have filed his complaint against the suspects to Ban Johnson who as American League President would have been an objective participant. Johnson would then have made a fair investigation. If convinced that the eight uncertain players were guilty, he would have to decide whether just to ban them from the American League or carry the case to a disinterested Garry Herrmann as Chairman of the National Commission. As this particular case involved an interleague World Series, he would have brought the case to Herrmann.

Garry would have conducted further investigation and, assuming the players guilt was established, "would have taken additional steps…"[183] The players, no doubt, would have been suspended from major league baseball. Herrmann would have passed his findings along to the leaders of the rest of "organized baseball." The "minor" or "independent" leagues receiving this information would also have been forced to make decisions regarding these ballplayers. Should they have agreed with Herrmann's decision, these leagues could have also agreed to ban the affected players. Had this sequence been followed, the players could have initiated "appeal processes" on many different levels. Those Black Sox desiring to continue to play baseball may well have received that opportunity on some level.

Had this discipline procedure been properly followed: the case of the "Black Sox" might never have moved to civil court, the careers of eight players may never have been ruined and the history of baseball certainly would have been altered. It seems that "personality conflicts and egos" blocked the way of early justice in this matter.

---

[183]   Ibid. 161.

# CHAPTER FOURTEEN

It was nearly a year before the "defecation" of the 1919 World Series would contact the "oscillator" of a Chicago grand jury. The proceedings were convened, ironically enough, to investigate allegations of those who felt something was "not right" regarding betting of some Chicago Cub games.[184] The specific game involving the "north siders" was one of August 31, 1920 against the Philadelphia Phillies. Cub president Bill Veeck Sr. reported that he had received two separate telephone calls indicating that this game would not be played "on the square." This manipulation would seem even more amazing when thought is given to the fact that the Cubs were in fifth place in the National League and the Phillies were eighth (last.)[185] These allegations were never proven. The legacy of this ballgame was that the grand jury did investigate. These charges would soon seem "small potatoes" compared to what the grand jury would eventually uncover. The Cubs and the Phillies would unwittingly bequeath "hell" upon the Chicago White Sox.

If the actions of those in power of the world of baseball in 1920 were any indication, baseball was hoping that the stigma of the 1919 World Series would "just go away." Investigations had been light and penalties non existent regarding any activities of October 1919. It would take the actions of a reporter, Hugh Fullerton of the Chicago Herald and Examiner to set events in motion.[186] Fullerton had never felt right about the events of the Series. Hugh responded with actions that required no small amount of courage. Fullerton interviewed both Jackson and

---

[184] "The Black Sox." available from http//www.Chicago's.org/history/black-sox/blk5.html. 1.

[185] Victor Luhrs. *THE GREAT BASEBALL MYSTERY: THE 1919 WORLD'S* SERIES. A. S. Barnes and Company. 1966. South Brunswick, N. J. 114.

[186] Ibid., 2.

Cicotte regarding their play in the Series. Both guilt ridden players admitted complicity with gamblers during the eight games. Fullerton convinced Jackson to testify before the grand jury. Mr. And Mrs. Cicotte would immediately determine that the only recourse was for Eddie to tell all he knew.[187] Perhaps the grand jury would be lenient.

The other Black Sox grasped the idea that little was to be gained by their continued silence. Underrepresented before the grand jury, each told everything they knew about "The fix." Since "Maranda" was still well in the future, the concept of "remaining silent" probably never crossed their minds.

On July 5, 1921 a "Bill of Particulars" was issued in THE CRIMMINAL COURT OF COOK COUNTY. In indictment number 23912 three groups of men were charged with conspiring to "make certain in advance of the playing of said games that the outcome thereof and the winner thereof, and so as to make certain in advance of the playing of all of the games of said series that the outcome of the majority of the games of said series and the winner of the majority of games in said series of games"[188] Among those conspired against was Charles C. Nims of Chicago. Sport Sullivan had fraudulently acquired $200,000 from Nims based upon the outcome of "said games." Here this author becomes confused. Gambling was illegal in both Illinois and Ohio. An individual who had placed an illegal bet involving an event could then sue because the outcome of that event had been maneuvered in a manner that he would lose illegal money? Apparently there was no ambiguity in the conducting of this combined illegal action, as the charges on behalf of Mr., Nims "stood."

The defendants were divided into three groups. Seven of the Chicago ballplayers were the first. Ironically, Fred McMullin was

---

187   Aainof, <u>EIGHT MEN OUT</u>. 171.
188   <u>http://www.law.umke.edu/caculty/projects.ftrials/blacksox/blacksoxparticulars.html</u>. 2.

originally indicted by the Grand Jury, but not prosecuted on the charges. While everyone agreed that Freddie was a member of the Black Sox, it was interesting that he was not included in the group that was brought "to trial." [189] Apparently the Prosecutors for the state of Illinois felt that Freddie's participation during the Series had been so inconsequential that charges would be useless. Freddie might have been disappointed not to be included with his friends. While he did not play often, there was never any doubt as to what color "Sox" the infielder "wore." The rest of "the boys" were left to "face the music." They had performed the "illegal" activity on the field. Their "conviction" would later come in the "court of Judge Landis."

It is somewhat disheartening that as a child this author collected baseball cards. While there was nothing sinister in this hobby for millions of youngsters, some of these efforts may have been misguided. The "legends" card of Kennesaw Mountain Landis referred to him as one who saved baseball after the "Black Sox Scandal." These words of heroism remained in the heart of at least one reader for nearly a lifetime. Looking back, these phrases may not have been the whole truth.

Landis had first made his reputation in court as a "Trust Busting" juror in the cases against Standard Oil in the first decade of the Twentieth Century. "The Judge" found this corporation guilty of 1,462 indictments and fined the corporation over twenty nine million dollars. This background would seem to make Landis an "impartial" leader in labor/management affairs and a perfect leader for the legally embattled business of baseball. A close evaluation would show, however that Standard Oil would pay only $1462.00 in fines "because of Landis' complete disregard for legality."[190] There can be no doubt that the theatrics of Landis had been loved by many Americans (including President

---

[189]    Luhrs. *THE GREAT BASEBALL MYSTERY: THE 1919 WORLD'S SERIES.* 185

[190]    Ibid. 200

Theodore Roosevelt who commented to Landis actions as "that's bully.") Still, one might like a more "even track record" from one who would change the lives of those over whom unquestioned authority would be exercised.

Victor Luhrs seems to have a fairly good perspective of Kennesaw Mountain Landis' judicial career: "In fact, come war or peace, most of Judge Landis' decisions were reversed, not through technicalities but for blatant disregard of common justice and common sense. He should have been removed from the bench for incompetence."[191] Eventually, the fate of talented but ignorant baseball players would be placed in these famous but erratic hands. On November 12, 1920 fifteen of the sixteen owners of major league baseball teams voted that "the Judge" be given unlimited power as "High Commissioner of Organized Baseball." In fairness to the club owners, this was not a plan "cooked up" to suit Judge Landis. The original concept to redesign baseball leadership had been put forth by Albert D. Laker, a minority owner of the Cubs. The idea had been to redesign the three member "Baseball Commission."[192] It had not been the original intention to give one man *"unlimited power."* Apparently in their eagerness to obtain a leader of the "stature" of KML baseball leadership had abandoned the thought of two other individuals to mitigate the power of the new "Commissioner." Phil Ball of the Browns abstained. [193] The reasons for Mr. Ball's moderate descent were not given. Had I been an owner, I would have questioned giving "unlimited power" to anyone!

At least one source believes that the vote was not nearly as lopsided as the tally would indicate. Under this arrangement Ban Johnson, President of the American League, would be reduced to a "mere figurehead"[194] under the authority of the Commissioner.

---

[191]  Ibid. 201.
[192]  Ibid. 203.
[193]  Ibid. 202.
[194]  Ibid. 204.

The five American League owners loyal to Johnson originally voted against the concept.[195] The issue that divided the American League ownership was "Carl Mays." Johnson had declared Mays a "free agent" from the St. Louis Browns after a contract dispute. Comiskey had put a claim in for the services of the right handed pitcher and lost. Charlie was then whole heartedly in favor of a Commissioner with the power to overrule the decisions of Johnson. The "border votes" of the league would eventfully "cave in" to the pressure of the majority. Perhaps the "abstention" of Ball was a protest regarding this matter. No matter how the political maneuvering is interpreted the score would appear to be: Comiskey and Landis "One": Johnson "Zero." While Ban Johnson would continue in his duties as "American League President" until his death, the value of his brilliance and innovation would be virtually eliminated. In life, as in the box score, the losses need be accounted for with as much attention as the wins!

The "court tests" of the wisdom and legality of such a move would not emerge for several decades. In the interim it was mostly a matter of "the Commissioner right or wrong but the Commissioner just the same." Because of (or perhaps in spite of) the leadership of the likes of Landis, Happy Chandler, Ford Frick et al, "America's Game" would evolve into a multi billion dollar business as the Twentieth Century unfolded.

The keepers of the "keys to Cooperstown" may have unlocked the doors for baseball's first commissioner, but a deeper look shows that a halo might have been ill fitting. The "canonizations" of ordinary men are often premature. The baseball equivalent of that process was bestowed upon an Illinois judge. His worthiness of such honor need be left to the judgment of each who has examined his credentials.

Such realizations as to the "warts" in the performance of KML are only concessions to the realities of adult life. Still, this

---

195    Ibid.

compromise of legend to fact as to the career of Judge Kennesaw Mountain Landis is yet another reason for sadness of the events surrounding the "law and justice" of baseball long ago.

In spite of the outcome of the proceedings, Gleason was an unsung hero. Honest during an "exhaustive cross examination" the Kid concluded. "I think they're the greatest ball club I've ever seen. Period."[196] Few could have said it better.

Bill Burns, Hal Chase and were grouped separately. This distinction was made because while the two had made their livings performing as ballplayers at a stage of their lives, they were not members of the 1919 White Sox. Joe Gedeon didn't even play in Chicago. Joe was a member of the *St Louis Browns.* Gideon was a friend of Chick Gandil's. Joe was apparently a "man of conscience." The St. Louis second baseman admitted publicly that he had bet on Cincinnati in the 1919 World Series based upon advice from his friend, the Chicago first baseman. It is difficult to determine how much the statements of Joe Gedeon affected the Chicago Grand Jury. It is easier to determine how these remarks affected the first Commissioner of Baseball. When the lifetime suspensions were bestowed upon players by Kennesaw Mountain Landis based upon the 1919 World Series, non participant Gedeon was included.

The third group was possibly the most interesting of all. For a lack of a better term we shall refer to them as "the gamblers." This aggregation was composed of: Joseph J. "Sport" Sullivan; Abe Attell (aka Rachael Brown); Carl Zook, Ben Franklin- no, not that one; Ben Levi; Louis Levi; and David Zelzer. Arnold Rothstein was not indicted. Interestingly enough, he would testify later as a concerned "sportsman."

AR must have made an interesting witness. Donald Henderson Clark wrote "His voice was mild and pleasing; his

---

[196] http://www.dvrbs.com/CamdenSports-KidGleason.htm. 10.

mannerisms graceful; his grammar was not perfect…and his wit was amazing."[197]

Rothstein saw himself more as a businessman than a gangster. "The essence of organized crime as perfected by Arnold Rothstein, was not structural organization as the conventional world knew it. It was, rather, the absence of structure. His office on West Fifty-Seventh Street dealt strictly with the legal side of his activities-his real estate investments, his Broadway shows, his racehorses. It would have been folly to allow a lawbreaker, or any evidence of his criminal activities, through his office doors.[198]

Arnold Rothstein was in the middle of a "great run that would end badly." Strangely enough of all his varied interests it was betting that would eventually "do him in."

"But Rothstein, the Brain, self-destructed. Gambling obsessed him and he bet compulsively, made huge bets, won some and lost more. In 1928 Rothstein played in one of Broadway's most fabulous poker games. One that lasted from September 8 to 10. At the end Rothstein was out $320,000. That Rothstein could lose shocked the wise guys of Broadway not nearly as much as the fact that Rothstein welched on the debt. He declared the game had been "fixed."[199] There was *that word* again. Ironic wasn't it?

On November 4, 1928 Arnold Rothstein was murdered in a New York hotel room. Although no one was ever convicted the primary suspects were the "winners" in the September card game. Imagine that! Arnold Rothstein who had tried so hard not to "live by the sword" died at the hands of the same weapon.

Under the rules prevailing at the time the Black Sox were not constitutionally deprived. Ben Short seems to have acted

---

[197]  http://www.crimelibrary.com/gangsters_outlaws/mob_bosses/rothstein/index_1.html. Accessed 9 October, 2005.

[198]  http://www.uncp.edu/home/haga/CRJ109620Big%620Names/tsld022.htm. 1. Accessed 9 October, 2005.

[199]  http://www.carpenoctem.tv/mafia/rothstein.html. 2. Accessed 9 October, 2005.

brilliantly for the defense. Another defense attorney Morgan Framberg uttered the statement that summed up the thoughts of many who had observed the proceedings. Speaking of Arnold Rothstein he inquired "Why was he not brought here? … Why were these underpaid ballplayers, these penny-ante gamblers who may have bet a few nickels on the World Series brought here to be goats in this case?"[200]

It should be noted that there was at least one "innocent victim" from the 1919 Chicago White Sox who had his career ended by the play of the 1919 World Series. Grover Lowdermilk was a "workmanlike" major league hurler for nine seasons. The pitcher retired after the 1920 season. It has been reported that Grover no longer had the "heart" to continue throwing. This could easily be the result of doubt regarding the concern for the efforts of those "behind the pitcher" to win any given game. The tragedy of 1919 continued to entwine unwitting participants.

---

[200]  http://www.law.umkc.edu/faculty/projuects/ftrials/blacksox/blacksoxaccount.html. 8. Accessed 8 July,2005

# CHAPTER FIFTEEN

I do believe that the accused would have benefited, from "day one" of the investigation to have been assisted by a union representative and an attorney advising them that it was not the obligation of the witness to make the investigation easier. If each of the players had displayed the memory of James Riddle Hoffa their plight could not possibly have become more severe.

At the actual trial the attorneys for the defense led by Ben Short appear to have done an admirable job of suppressing references to the now absent confessions and making the best of a disordered legal situation.[201] Some bad blood surfaced during the hearings. St Louis Brown's player Joe Gideon testified that his friend Risberg wired coded instructions on how to bet the games of the Series. It is not clear that Gideon and Risberg remained friends after the trial. There was the legendary "alleged" threat to Jackson by the Swede. If true, one could understand Jackson "running scared." These signs of lack of unity must have driven Short and the rest of the defense team nearly crazy. The best tribute to the defense team was that the defendants were ruled "not guilty." A Grand Jury in 1920 could not have ruled that the defendants must be allowed to continue their lives as though they were innocent.

In some ways the demise of these ballplayers was the result of an "oft told fish story…" Charles Comiskey and Ban Johnson were largely responsible for building the American League together. The two had once shared an office in Chicago. When the League was formed from the ashes of the "Old Western League" Comiskey had supported Johnson for both the job of President

---

[201] "The Black Sox Trial, An Account." Douglas A. Linder. 2001. http://www.law.umke.edu.edu/faculty/projects/trials/blacksox/blacksoxaccount.html. Accessed 8 July, 2005.

and a position on the Board of Governors that ruled the game in the days prior to the selection of a commissioner.

For all of his talents, it is reported that Johnson did his job as American League President with "…little grace and ill humor. Johnson was hot-tempered, bullheaded imperious and uncompromising, not unlike many other tycoons of his time. But he was successful."[202]

Ban and Charlie became embroiled in a dispute regarding several league rulings that had gone against the White Sox. Principle among these was a decision that caused Chicago to lose pitcher Jack Quinn to the Yankees. This was no small loss as Quinn would compete in the major leagues for twenty three years and win two hundred forty seven games. At some point during this discussion the owner of the White Sox was reported to have roared "I made you, and by God I'll break you."[203]

At the time the matters separating Comiskey and Johnson seemed small. During the winter months "the Old Roman" departed to his fishing lodge in Wisconsin. While there, Comiskey caught several magnificent trout. He carefully iced and packed two of his prizes and dispatched them to Ban's office as a "peace offering."[204] A delay in shipping melted the ice. By the time the package arrived in Chicago the contents were, well, disgusting. It seemed at though the two men were no longer friends. Ban Johnson perceived the gesture as an insult and the two would go to their graves hating each other.

It was unfortunate for Comiskey that Ban was the president of his league during the 1919 World Series. It has been widely reported that after the conclusion of the first game of the Series Kid Gleason spoke to Charlie of the strong possibility that "the

---

[202]  http://www.baseballlibrary.com/baseballlibrary/ballplayers/J/Johnson_ Ban.stm. Accessed 1 October 2005. 1.

[203]  . Ibid. 2. Accessed 2 October, 2005.

[204]  Jackson, Joseph Jefferson and Furman Bisher. "This is the Truth." http:// www.law.umke.edu/faculty/prouects/ftrials/Jackson/jacksonstory.html.4.

fix was on." Comiskey duly conveyed this information to John Heydler President of the National League. Charlie obviously felt that he was in a better position to communicate with Heydler than with the President of his own league. He was right! When Heydler relayed the information to Ban Johnson, the American League President responded that Comiskey's information was "The yelp of a beaten cur." [205] Thus, personal antagonism had ruined the last real chance to nip the "Black Sox Scandal" in "the bud." Lives might have been changed if Johnson's hatred of Comiskey had not colored his ability to do his job as American League President. After this opportunity, the "goose was cooked" for all involved in this tragedy.

Johnson was still President of the American League at the time that "the White Sox Grand Jury" met in Chicago. To that point the League President had been strongly opposed to the creating of a Commissioner for the sport, no doubt feeling that it would reduce his authority. During "the scandal" Johnson reversed that position campaigning for the selection of Landis. Ban no doubt made it clear to the Judge his position on the "issue in Chicago." It is clear that KML acted as Johnson would have wished. Perhaps, an "old debt" was repaid. Certainly, Comiskey's team was devastated. The real losers, of course, were the ballplayers. Eight men had their professional lives ruined. How's that for "a kettle of fish"?

Those who defend Joseph Jefferson Jackson in particular and the Black Sox in general often claim "They were never indicted or convicted of anything." This I would argue before Judge Landis as the union representative for "the guys." The lack of conviction was, at best, tenuous. Certain critical records were missing from the grand jury transcripts for about three years.[206] History has attributed the disappearance to the actions of a man

---

[205] Luhrs. ***THE GREAT BASEBALL MYSTERY: THE 1919 WORLD SERIES.*** 149.

[206] Ibid, 286.

who strongly resembled an acquaintance of a Chicago associate of one Arnold Rothstein and the reappearance to the connections of one Charles A. Comiskey.[207] Still, by the time the records were uncovered in 1923, the players should have been back on the ball field and the records should have been downplayed to a "footnote."

Joe Jackson's days as a phenomenal baseball player were almost over. Over his thirteen season major league career Jackson hit .356. This mark was within striking distance of Ty Cobb's all time mark of .367. Jackson once hit an amazing .408 for an entire season. While batting standards have changed greatly in the modern era, some measure of this accomplishment would be that no one has hit better than .400 since 1941.

Since 1919 Jackson has become an even greater legend as an "innocent victim" in the Black Sox scandal. When newly appointed baseball commissioner Kenesaw Mountain Landis barred eight Chicago White Sox players from baseball "forever" because of the 1919 World Series it made no difference to him what players had participated. Those who "knew" and had done nothing were also guilty. Bucky Weaver was included in this area. Many observers believed that Jackson should have been as well. In his confession before the Chicago Grand Jury Jackson denied being "in the conspiracy."[208] This was a position that Jackson would maintain until his death in 1951.

"Shoeless Joe" would later contend that Risberg had made physical threats against him to attempt to compel his silence before the grand jury. It was in this matter that Jackson would issue his famous quote "the Swede's a hard guy." This was quite a compliment considering the company the Minnesotan was keeping! Risberg would, of course deny the accusation. Who knows? No charges were ever brought forth from the incident.

---

[207] Ibid, 286.
[208] Asinof, *EIGHT MEN OUT,* 290.

Eliot Asinof asserted that Joe attempted to meet with Charles
Comiskey the day after the World Series ended to confess his portion of the scheme. Such a rendezvous might well have cleared
the air and saved the "skins" of the Black Sox. Comiskey was too
busy, according to this report, to see Jackson. Shoeless Joe went
home for the winter. Apparently the urge to unburden himself
passed in the off season. A grand jury confession signed by a
man who could neither read nor write would soon be forthcom-
ing. Jackson may not have been innocent, but he certainly was
abused.

Early in this presentation I mention that "The Fix" was a
labor action gone bad. I am not an attorney but do have some
years experience as a labor representative. In that context, let me
offer a few thoughts that certainly couldn't have hurt these ballplayers beginning with events of September, 1920.

Labor had made great sacrifices for "the War Effort" beginning with the European portion of that conflict in 1914. The
government had obtained a "no strike" pledge from labor leadership. While the affect had not been universally successful, work
stoppages had been extremely rare during World War One.
Industries considered essential to the production of materials
needed in Europe had increased production with very little monetary advance for the workers. A grateful government had placed
American Federation of Labor President Samuel Gompers on *the
Post War Reconstruction Board.* While Sam cared little for unskilled
labor, he certainly had the US President's attention. We would
have lobbied heavily for "our leader" to petition Washington D.
C. for "forgiveness." Weren't productive ballplayers preferable to
unemployed journeymen?

It is not known how much the senators and representatives
from Illinois were "badgered" regarding this situation. We would
have written and visited these men (all men at the time) to the
point that they would have woke up in the middle of the night
screaming "Weaver and Jackson are not guilty!" Simultaneous

with these efforts would be contacts with delegates from: South Carolina, Pennsylvania, Michigan, Minnesota, Wisconsin, Missouri, Kansas and California. These were the states that the players called "home." How could elected officials from these domains let their citizens be abused so?

Conversations should have been especially interesting with those from South Carolina. Joe Jackson was, perhaps, the most famous member of their state. In many ways he possessed all of the virtues of a "soft, southern culture." How could the elected representatives of this state continue to let the northern press vilify Joe as an "ignorant hillbilly"? Was Jackson's lack of "northern expertise" particularly literacy a reason to allow the continued portrayal of the citizens of South Carolina as a "bunch of country bumpkins"? I doubt that the educated aggregation in Washington was greatly amused.

"Senator Dial, didn't you come from beginnings nearly as humble as those of Joe Jackson? Joe never learned to read or write, but neither did a lot of other people. Jackson returned home all those winters after the season was over to be back among the home folks. We're letting a bunch of northern lawyers hang one of our own." This would be dramatic, but also accurate. At some point deep in the conversation it would be pointed out that standing up for Joe Jackson would be a politically popular move. Such action could not help but gain him additional respect from party leaders "back home." Dial must have already known that he was in political trouble in South Carolina. He would not be denominated by the Democratic Party for a second term. Most politicians believe in surviving to fight another day. Such a tactic might have helped one South Carolina voter. At this point in time help for one of the Black Sox could be equated with help for them all.

"Senator Smith, Joe made a lot of money in the north, but he and his wife continued to own and run the store in Carolina. From the time he was a kid in the mills he was paying 'South

Carolina' taxes. What have those people in Illinois ever done for us? Are we going to leave the greatest ballplayer we've ever produced alone to swing at the end of a northern rope? This doesn't seem like a very good job of sticking up for our own."

The "eye of the storm" had been in Illinois. The White Sox home base was there. Charles Comiskey paid big taxes to the state. Judge Landis held court there. The grand jury had met in Chicago. The revenue that baseball generated was far more than "ticket sales." Sportswriters, vendors, gamblers (obviously they were present,) transportation specialists and, yes even politicians, made "hay" when the Sox played baseball. Each of these portions would certainly be of concern to the elected officials of "the Land of Lincoln."

"Senator McCormick, exactly who benefits if the Sox attendance drops to the level of that of the Cubs? Do you have any idea how much revenue the state would lose if no one decides to come to Comiskey Park?" This idea could be reinforced by the selective boycotts during the 1921 season.

"Senator McKinley, the state has already received a tremendous 'black eye' from this entire incident. Would it not make the most sense to 'cut the losses' bring the players back to work and to try to put the entire incident behind us?"

"Congressman Copley, you call yourself 'Progressive'? One of your constituents (Weaver, a resident of Illinois) has just been 'lynched.' Shouldn't something be done to prevent 'frontier justice' in this case?" A world of "good guys and bad guys" is naïve. Most everyone opens their eyes in the morning and tries to do the best they can with the day they have been given. The Black Sox were no exception. Ordinary men who placed themselves in an extremely bad situation. Still, if there was an innocent victim among "the eight" it was Weaver. My research has found no opinion that Bucky gave anything less than his best effort in the 1919

World Series. The primary "sin" attributed to the third baseman was that he refused to "rat on his buddies." In many quarters this would have been considered an admirable characteristic.

As we consider Weaver we must be moved by the words of Nelson Algren. "Don't bring up Buck Weaver or how he looked the last time you saw him. Begging a reporter six months out of high school to clear his name so he could play again. 'I'll play for nothing, tell 'em. Just one season, tell 'em.'"[209] Any elected official who would not respond to that type of a plea would never get my vote again.

"Representative Rainey, citizens of Illinois, duly sworn as a 'Grand Jury' brought no charges forth against the ballplayers. How can the executives of baseball ignore the findings of people who vote in Illinois elections and do what they 'damned well please'? Grand Juries may as well cease to exist in the state if the sports leaders can do anything they like after the state has gone to all of the time and expense to determine the lack of guilt."

We would have promised the Illinois delegation that if Bucky was not allowed to return to the field we would haunt them forever. After all, Weaver, Cicotte and Jackson felt that they had been "promised" by Comiskey that they would be reinstated if they were not convicted on charges in civil court. This commitment was later countermanded by the new "High and Exalted Ruler of Baseball," its first Commissioner- Landis.

"Is there no value in a verbal contract in the state of Illinois? If we don't get the reinstatement job done in our lifetimes, we won't even let succeeding generations forget what you have done to these men. Your elected successors will pray for peace and wish you had brought justice to this matter many years ago.

In our efforts to portray the vindication of the players as a "never ending struggle, we would have been very close to correct. Marjorie Follett of Pontiac Illinois was Weaver's niece. She

---

[209] Asinof. *EIGHT MEN OUT.* 279.

died in October of 2003 after dedicating much of her adult life to clearing the name of her uncle. To the end she was optimistic that the third baseman would one day be cleared. Her movement had been brightened when baseball Commissioner Bud Selig had agreed to do further investigation into the Peter Rose matter. Chicago sports historian Jerome Holzman was Selig's designee to look into the Weaver matter. Follett operated a website www.ClearBuck.com. To date the desired results have not been achieved. This would, however, advise those in Washington D. C. that opposing the Black Sox (and their memories) would be a long struggle.

Next we would move on to Eddie Cicotte's home state of Michigan. It should be noted that during "the Roaring Twenties" this all republican group might well be a "tough sell." Still, "Michiganders" were Eddie's people and we would not let his elected representation forget it.

"Senator Couzens, for his entire career Eddie was making money in Detroit, Boston and Chicago and bringing it home to spend in Michigan. 'Knuckles' was helping your economy with whatever disposable income he had available. He probably would have brought more back except that he was paid so pathetically. During his entire career no one ever lifted a finger to help him make a living wage as a ballplayer. Doesn't it seem about time that he did get some help?"

"What Eddie was doing, Congressman Ketchum, was attempting to keep his farm solvent. He made the majority of his money in Boston, Detroit and Chicago, but he brought it back home. Michigan was his base of operations. His loves were there- Michigan land and his Michigan wife. The loves are still there. Can't we do something to help pay him back for the years that he dedicated to the state?"

"Senator Newberry, we don't have to tell you that times are hard for farmers. You're hearing that from folks all over the state. Eddie's run as a celebrity baseball player was almost over. All he wanted from the 1919 World Series was to be sure that he kept his land instead of the bank. The place would have been paid for if Comiskey had treated him right in the first place. Charlie's still running his million dollar business and Eddie's out of work, what's just about that? I know that your job is not to 'dispense fairness' but every once in a while you have to stand up and say 'this is wrong.' I'm sure that if you do this the voters in Michigan will never forget what side you are on!"

When we approached the Minnesota people about Arnold "Chick" Gandil our problem would be complicated. The first two strikes against the first baseman were: Chick masterminded "the fix" and he didn't seem one bit sorry about it. Prior to the 1920 season Gandil and Comiskey had become embroiled in yet another contract dispute. At this point he had become a former ballplayer, turning his interests to his rodeo and cowboy careers. The game had always been about the money for Chick and he had made his "big score." Excluding the other members of the Black Sox few people seemed to "like" Chick. A "hard luck story" wasn't going to work here. Putting aside these personal prejudices and approaching the matter as a labor representative should, it was time to put the best effort possible forth in favor of Gandil.

"Senator Kellogg, Chick was just trying to make a living. Comiskey was paying 'starvation wages' and the players had already taken too much from the rich man. As we have seen since the 1919 World Series story was made public, there were not a whole lot of other options available. Why do we believe that the players should have any particular loyalty to Comiskey and the White Sox? I believe that subsequent events have shown that baseball cared nothing for your 'native son' nor any other of these players."

"Don't you think, Senator Nelson, that these players have

already suffered enough? The suspensions that they have suffered have thus far permanently ruined their reputations and left them scrambling to make a living. Chick has been gone from the game for several years now. It is doubtful that he would want to return to this career, anyway. A *lifetime suspension* from doing anything in organized baseball is excessive. If someday he would like to 'umpire in the Texas League' it would seem that this opportunity should be open to him. Justice has already been served. It is time for some humanity in this matter as well."

We might have hit "pay dirt" in Hap's home state of Wisconsin. One of the senators of that state was Robert M. La Follette Sr. This man was a Republican who lived is life by progressive values. He would, in fact, amass almost five million votes as the Progressive Party candidate for President of the United States in 1924. This total was nearly one sixth of all the votes cast.[210] Quite impressive, one would think, for a candidate from an independent party.

La Follette believed that there was a constant struggle between "the people" and the "selfish interests" for control of the government. In 1908 during debate of the Aldrich-Vineland Currency Act La Follette argued that the nations economy was dominated in its entirety by fewer than one hundred men.[211] It would seem reasonable to believe that this powerful senator would be closer in sympathy with the Black Sox than with millionaire Charles Comiskey.

"Senator La Follette, I have never seen anyone approach their work with the joy that Happy Felsch brought to the baseball diamond. It has been said that he would play for free. I believe this, because it's just about what Charles Comiskey has had him doing for the past several seasons.

According to the baseball 'Reserve Clause' after a player

---

[210]  "La Follette, Robert M(arion) available from http://search.eb.com/elections/micro/333/3html. 3. Accessed 16 July 2005.

[211]  Ibid. 2.

signs with a team he 'belongs to them *forever*. One moment in a man's entire lifetime binds him for eternity. The club, on the other hand, can sell, trade or demote this man at their pleasure. I thought slavery went out with the Civil War. If I'd been Felsch, they would have called me 'Grumpy.' What the players did wasn't right- but what else could they do? Baseball has not been a particularly 'clean' business, anyway. The suspensions have already lingered long enough. Do Something! Landis says he'll resign if the players are reinstated- let him. There are a lot of good men who could do the commissioner's job. Bob Jr. still looking for work? Wouldn't that be a 'kick'? 'Liberal Republican runs baseball.' One giant leap for the working man!

If you can't garner enough votes to mandate the reinstatement of the Black Sox, you could always use the Senate's unlimited filibuster. How many days do you think the owners of the baseball teams would want to see their 'dirty laundry' hung in public before they screamed for mercy and wanted to make an immediate deal?"

"We have been working with Senator La Follette to try to get some help for these guys, Congressman Beck, but we *really* need your help as well. These guys are basically farm kids, just like you. Happy Felsch was only sticking with his friends getting into this mess in the first place. Most of the deal was based on keeping Eddie Cicotte's farm in Michigan. Sure, the guys were wrong; but big business is trying to bury them. All we are asking is that the Black Sox get a 'fair shake.' They need a chance to continue in some capacity in the sport that they have given so much to."

"Senator James Alexander Reed of the 'Show Me State.' Let me show you what baseball is doing to Missourian Claude Williams. Lefty is already saddled with the dubious record of the most losses in baseball World Series history. After his experience with 'the Old Roman' and the White Sox he left baseball nearly broke. Williams was never allowed to reach his peak years in the sport. Now they're telling him that he can't even be employed in baseball."

"Representative Rucker, tell me that Lefty doesn't have enough talent to remain in baseball. Hell, he'd be a star (the word superstar was generations away) with the Browns. What a waste of talent. 'America's game' should be available to those who do it best. The best talent should be viewed by the customer- just like on Broadway. Put Lefty back to work. Tell baseball that those in Washington not Comiskey and Landis protect both employees and customers." I would not mention that it was a pleasure to finally speak with Democrats. Bob La Follette aside, the GOP has not traditionally been fond of the ordinary laborer.

In California we would be fighting legend as much as fact. As Joe Jackson summarized "The Swede was a hard guy."[212] We are asking for compassion for another man who was not famous for kindness. Being stoic had done Risberg no good. Being tough was a virtue for a baseball player of his era. This style would hurt a now forcibly retired Charles August Risberg. Oh well, we're not running a candidate for "Miss Congeniality" let's get to work.

"There is no question that the Swede was a great player. It appears, Senator Shortridge, that this Californian is being punished more for his lack of communication skills and education than for what happened in 1919. Maybe they should have just sent the guys to jail for a while and then let them play on parole. They were never convicted of anything. What does the law say about 'beyond a reasonable doubt.'?

"Since when, Senator Johnson is being 'tough' a crime. The shortstop would be in better shape if he had been a 'popular wimp.' They can't think that differently in the east. We're all talking English here, let the ballplayers play."

---

[212]   Asinof. EIGHT MEN OUT. 209.

Next we would speak with the folks from Kansas. "This was the one most expensive at bat in the history of baseball. Senator Curtis, Freddie McMullin didn't have one thing to do with how the 1919 World Series came out. While it has been alleged that he acted as a "courier" between the players and the gamblers[213] even this role meant nothing. Do you think Abe Attel or Chick Gandil would trust the vital details of plan and payment to someone who played such a small role in the plot? Your voter was guilty of only one thing, remaining loyal to his friends."

"Senator Capper, tell me about the constitutionality using information overheard in a bathroom to determine how a player participates in a baseball game. Freddie McMullin's contribution to the 1919 Series meant nothing. It's like sending someone to the electric chair for jaywalking. Can't you do *something*?"

As we asked for help, we would look for more help. Did these representatives know of the labor supporters in congress who might help with such a cause? Were there "human rights advocates" (a term that would not come into vogue for many more years) looking for a cause? Representatives facing close elections who might want the opportunity to speak and write in order to "look good for the home folks"? We would care little of party or special interests, we would be looking for "life jackets."

Our final goal would be a "sense of congress" resolution that the Black Sox be forgiven for their transgressions and allowed to continue their careers. Winning such a vote would have been difficult. The immediate plan would be to "officially" put the situation to the American public. One elected official from each house would have been enough to "bring the matter to the floor." Once again we would be applying "political pressure" to Landis and Comiskey. Who knows, searching like Dioganese, we might

---

213  Luhrs. *THE GREAT BASEBALL MYSTERY: THE 1919 WORLD SERIES.* 144.

have found enough honest men, willing to help, to perform a miracle.

# CHAPTER SIXTEEN

The Chicago Federation of Labor was a compelling force on behalf of the workers of this era. Contact with the leaders of this movement would have been a necessity. "The guys" were, most of all abused employees. Who were the leaders of the CFL and why might they have helped? To answer these questions, we must first know something of John J. Fitzpatrick and William Z. Foster.

John J. Fitzpatrick was born in Athione, Ireland (circa 1871) and was brought to Chicago by an uncle after his parents died. He worked in a brass factory and at the Stockyards before learning to horseshoe. He became a union member of what was to become the "International Union of Journeymen horseshoers of the United States and Canada." Fitzpatrick was president of the CFL from 1900 to 1901 and again from 1906-46. In short, he was the "main man" in Chicago labor just when eight desperate Black Sox needed him most.[214] "Schooled in the craft oriented pragmatism of American labor, Fitzpatrick nevertheless harbored a deep sympathy for the immigrant workingmen of Chicago."[215] Fitzpatrick had originally proposed the organizational drive in Chicago steel. It would be hoped that this sympathy and drive could also be felt for Chicago ballplayers.

With any luck, and the Black Sox certainly had received little enough of that, Fitzpatrick would have brought William Z. Foster on board with him. Foster's parents were "poor immigrants" his father was from Ireland and his mother from England.[216] This unusual combination could not have hurt William as he devel-

---

[214] "Fitzpatrick, John J." available from http://www.history.umd.edu/Gompers/glossary.htm. 4. Accessed 18 April, 2006.

[215] Brody, David. *LABOR IN CRISIS: THE STEEL STRIKE OF 1919."* The University of Illinois Press. Urbana, Illinois and Chicago. 1965. 62.

[216] Mazellis, Fred. "The Life of William Z. Foster." available from http://www.wsws.org/public_html/prioriss/iwb2-12/foster.htm. 1. Accessed 18 April, 2006.

oped the "fighting spirit" that he would need as a life long labor activist. The legendary Samuel Gompers saw Foster as one who "could be a real service to the cause of labor. He was a man of ability, a man of good presence, gentle in expression."[217]

Foster would become a communist at about the time the defense of the eight Chicago players should have been being built. Before Joseph McCarthy's "Red Scare" this was not an "unpardonable sin" in the United States. We should remember that we were speaking of the "Foster" of the 1915-1925 era. This man was a labor activist who happened to be a communist. Later it seemed that William V. would submerge his other visions in effort to protect his communist beliefs from the onslaught of the Cold War. Politics aside, Joe Jackson et al should have taken their friends where they might find them in 1921. William Z. Foster could have been a powerful friend! Foster was "a slight, soft spoken, intense man in his late thirties"[218] (in 1919.) William Z. was a veteran organizer first for the Carmen's Union and later on behalf of the unions in steel. Foster had played a major role in the steel strike of 1919. William Z. was the secretary of the National Committee for Organizing Iron and Steel Workers during that dispute.[219] In short, Foster had been through "the labor wars." If baseball wanted to play "hard ball," Foster had experience. It might well be that Landis and the club owners would rather reinstate eight "errant" players than face the prospect of Foster operating in their midst.

There is little doubt that the baseball hierarchy would have responded to any organizational effort in the same manner that U. S. Steel had pioneered. "We don't discharge men for belong-

---

[217]   Brody. *LABOR IN CRISIS.* 136.
[218]   David Brody. *LABOR IN CRISIS: THE STEEL STRIKE OF 1919.* The University of Illinois Press, Urbana, Illinois and Chicago. 1965. 62.
[219]   Ibid.

ing to a union," one of their officials was quoted as saying, "but, of course, we discharge men for agitating in the mills."[220]

Baseball management could have used the same logic, saying such as "We don't discharge players for seeking a union, but we do terminate based upon poor performance." Some might have believed unless the terminated player was Ty Cobb or Babe Ruth or JOE JACKSON. Foster had come across these problems before and could have had some success in dealing with these difficulties. "Do the words 'Federal League' still ring a bell KML?"

It has been pointed out that as well as being athletes, baseball players are entertainers. This would create an interesting link with another labor organization in Chicago: The International Association of Theatrical and Stage Employees (IATSE) operated its Local #2 from the "Windy City." Only Local #1 established in the "Broadway venue" of New York was a longer standing affiliate of this union. This would have been a logical association for our performers to form an alliance with. We would have tried to convince their leadership of the "entertainment theory." Should we be successful, we would have made the assertion that the suspensions were "discipline" (it would be hard to argue that a "lifetime suspension" was anything less than a termination.) Unions representing disciplined employees would certainly contend that such actions were subject to "a grievance procedure." The Black Sox would be more than willing to become dues paying members of a group dedicated to the project that would "...organize within its jurisdiction workers employed within the entertainment industry." Conversely, an entry into this portion of the entertainment industry would have given IATSE a forty year head start over other unions in organizing efforts in this entertainment field.

There may have been much promise in becoming aligned with an organization that prided itself in the continuing struggle against management. (We) ....were not all that different than our

---

220   Ibid. 89.

brethren working in the stockyards, steel mills or coal mines (or perhaps on the ball fields-tea) who had to cope daily with management/owners willing to exploit their circumstances. Those standing up in defiance of such ruthless tactics were soon forgotten. Uprisings quelled businessmen would revert back to their business…"[221]

It should be noted that the stated purpose of the International Alliance of Theater and Stage Employees is with: "…a core belief that our total membership is greater in strength than its individual members." It would be possible that those holding such beliefs might well be willing to help eight isolated entertainers/laborers in an effort to escape the island upon which they had been placed in effort to return them to the mainstream and continue their previous careers. "Hey Chuck, KML, WE ARE NO LONGER ALONE!

Becoming IATSE members would have legitimized any efforts that Fitzpatrick and Foster might have desired to make on behalf of members of a local within their federation. The theatrical and stage employees of Chicago also had a qualified and experienced staff that could have stood beside the ballplayers. A possible disruption to the entertainment industry in the second largest city in the country might well have given our grievants an access to a much wider national forum than one they could have ever imagined as their activities were confined predominantly to the "sports page" of the nation's newspapers.

The whole history of baseball could have been changed if organizational efforts had begun forty years before Marvin Miller attempted to lead the players "from the labor wilderness." It certainly would have been an interesting topic to discuss with Landis over a cup of coffee as he was so sanctimoniously proclaiming that the Black Sox would never play professional baseball again.

---

[221]    "IATSE Local 2: History." Available from http://iatselocal2.com/history/history.shtml. 1. Accessed 4 May, 2006.

If our dispute had continued until 1926, and should baseball decide not to "settle," we would have been certain that the "grievance" was still alive, we would have made use of a "new" influential friend. In that year radio station WCFL was launched in Chicago. This media outlet would pride itself for the next fifty two yeas[222] as being "the voice of labor in Chicago." This outlet began as a "listener supported station emphasizing labor and public affairs programming."[223] By 1926 it was already becoming a bit late to salvage the careers of the Black Sox. Such reclamation would not be impossible, particularly for Risberg and Williams. We might have been able to get Weaver his "one more year." This season would have made the third baseman "Hall of Fame" eligible.

By the date of the launching of this radio station, however, the emphasis would have shifted from the reinstatement of our players to active major league rosters to a struggle against the "lifetime" portion of their suspensions. How would the public of Chicago react to a reminder that "Shoeless Joe" could not coach in the Southern League? Would these same people be pleased with an account of the magnificent Buck Weaver walking the streets with holes in his shoes? Some listeners might have been moved to action. This would be another step in the battle to stop major league baseball from forgetting the contributions of the Chicago "Black Sox." The public was continuing to hear only one side of the story: "the guys in the 'white hats' were returning purity to the game. We would invest time, effort and money to assure that "the Voice of Labor" told the workers of Chicago of the suffering of athletic laborers at the hands of management.

The public would fall in love with the voices received in their living room by electronic transmission. The Chicago Federation of Labor was perceptive enough to take advantage of this

[222] Nathan Godfried. *WCFL CHICAGO'S VOICE OF LABOR 1926-78.* University of Illinois Press. Urbana, Illinois and Chicago. 1997. Cover.
[223] Ibid. XV.

phenomenon almost immediately. We would use every friend that we had within the Chicago Labor movement to assure that the plight of the ballplayers was placed in front of the public "nightly" if possible. No, I didn't say "if practical" the operative words would be "if possible."

We would have "targeted" Labor Day, Monday September 5, 1921 on our calendar. We would have sent an S.O.S. to labor leaders across the country. "Come support eight ill educated and underpaid laborers (the ballplayers) against the rich management "czars," owner (Comiskey) and the dictatorial Chairman of the Board (Landis.)

We would have invited major labor leaders from all over the country. Many would have declined, but some would have accepted. The publicity from such an adventure could not help but provide a boost for each of their own operations.

"Let's see if we can get John L. Lewis to put in an appearance. The United Mine Workers are just about the most dynamic unskilled group the world has ever known. The prestige of having this union's president in Chicago to help would be overwhelming. We would have the attention of 'the country.' Nobody has ever been bored at a Lewis speech."

"While we are dealing with those concerned with mining, is Mary Harris Jones still living in Illinois? I know she's 'the miner's angel' but she also knows how to raise hell. The sight of that ninety something pound woman standing up to the authorities of Chicago would be worth the 'price of admission.' I'll bet if we could get her up here we could draw quite a crowd!"

"Debs still in prison?" We believe that Eugene V. Debs' 1921 pardon had been completed by Labor Day. "Does he feel like challenging the minds of the American Public again yet? A world traveled Mid Westerner might feel right at home with what we're planning. See if he can show up!"

"Get in touch with the AFL. Pleasantly inquire as to Sam Gompers' health. If he's not doing anything Labor Day, invite him out! Mention that Lewis and Debs might be here. At least we'll have his attention."

"Clarence Darrow represented both Debs and Bill Haywood. Do you think he would be interested in coming to the party? Talking legalities to 'the guys.' He might just love the publicity. His legal advice couldn't hurt and his 'celebrity status' certainly would draw attention.

...And so it would go. Frank Duffy, America's labor representative at the 1919 Paris Peace Conference would give a dignified and diplomatic presence at the gathering...[224] John Phillip Frey, editor of the Iron Molders' Union of North America's newspaper. The written publicity from labor tabloids could have a positive spill over into the private press.

Adolph F. Germer of the UAW's district 12 headquartered in downstate Belleville, Illinois could add to Lewis' presence and would not have a long commute.

William Levi Hutcheson of the United Brotherhood of Carpenters and Joiners of America would also add "a diplomatic touch." Hutcheson had been a member of the War Labor Conference Board[225] and certainly would still have "contacts in Washington." An invitation to our "Labor Day Party" would be a certainty for Bill.

"John Brown Lennon of the Journeymen Tailors Union of North America is familiar with Illinois, having lived in Bloomington. I wonder if he's a White Sox fan. He's been a member of the U.S. Commission on Industrial Relations and a Commissioner of Conciliation for the United States Department

---

[224] http://www.history.umd.edu/Gompers/glossary.htm. Accessed 18 April, 2006. 2.

[225] Ibid. 8.

of Labor. Once again, Midwest background, Washington contacts. See if he'd like to come out."

"Daniel Joseph Tobin of the Teamsters is from Indianapolis, not a long trip. The National Civic Federation background will certainly qualify him as 'mainstream.' The 'teamsters' are already powerful and have some 'pull' in this country. Chicago and this type of a gathering may be perfect for Tobin."[226]

"As a founder of Hull House and a leader of the Amalgamated Clothing Workers Union Ellen Gates Starr is well known in this, her home town. She founded the Chicago Woman's Trade Union League[227] and would surely draw some women to our get together. See if she'd like to attend."

Not wanting to violate city ordinance, we would apply for a "Labor Day Parade" permit. The route that we would select would include the area directly in front of KML's office and that of Comiskey Park. We would ask the right for an assembly at a nearby city park at the conclusion of our journey.

I can visualize each member of the Chicago City Council choking on his (they were all of that gender at this point) cigar as they contemplated their quandary. Could the "city of Haymarket Square" stand such a demonstration? More important, could the "city of Broad Shoulders" refuse the opportunity for such a parade to the laboring constituents of their jurisdiction? The "path of least resistance" would dictate giving us our "little parade and park space." Should this not be granted, we expect to contact every labor sympathetic newspaper editor and reporter in the country to express "outrage" and support for our "Black Sox." We expect that the city council would get the message! Hey guys, does anybody have any influence with Charles Comiskey or Kennesaw Mountain Landis? All that our eight men want to do is play ball! Can you be of any help?

---

226   Ibid. 18.
227   Ibid.

# CHAPTER SEVENTEEN

Understanding that our "quest for justice" had only begun, additional help would be sought. I would have brought a "Marvin Miller" in to deal with the legal aspects of the problem. In addition a "David Fehr" would have dealt with the public relations aspect. While these gentlemen were several decades away from center stage in "the sports headlines, several individuals with combined talents almost as great as these men could have been employed. There was plenty of work to do. Someone would have argued to suppress the confession of our illiterate client. Chick Gandil would have been given instructions to leave sunny California for Illinois only under the order of subpoena. "All here this: We understand that we are playing in the 'big leagues' of the legal spectrum but we are no longer 'naked and afraid.'"

"Miranda Rights" were more than four decades away. "Weingarten Rights" were even further in the future. The Fifth Amendment was, however, in place. We would argue that the rights of this amendment had been violated for the ballplayers.

We would contend that Comiskey's refusal to meet with Jackson in October, 1919 and his "high handed" suspensions a year later indicated complicity as an "accessory after the fact" in the events of the 1919 World Series. It is almost certain that the authorities who were in charge of baseball at this juncture would have reduced player punishment rather than subject one of the "shining lights" among its ownership to close scrutiny regarding his activities during a scandal.

In order to properly represent my "grievant" I would have to bring up a word that club owners hated worse than "gambling." The magic word would have been "union." Unionism in baseball was nearly a half century away and very difficult to achieve at that late date. Who is to say that such a movement would ever meet with any success? On the other hand, who would have thought that John L. Lewis could be of any help to a bunch of illiterate miners?

In 1919 the International Workers of the World "the Wobblies" was nearing the end of a brief but rather successful era of organizing unskilled labor groups throughout the world. In the article "One Big Union- One Big Strike: The Story of the Wobblies" the author summarizes this movement. "Early in the 20th Century, the Industrial Workers of the World, called the 'Wobblies,' organized thousand of immigrant and unskilled workers in the United States. The Union eventually failed, but helped shape the modern American labor movement"[228]

It would seem that a situation such as the Blacksox could have been a political miracle for William Haywood, Joseph Ettor and the leadership of the IWW. This would have been a "cause" just when the light of the International Workers of the World was becoming a fading light. Admittedly, "the Wobblie plate" was rather full in 1919. In 1918 Haywood and the leadership had been convicted of "obstruction of the war effort" in federal court in Chicago. The appeals were in process; eventually the convictions would be upheld. It would seem that defending a group of downtrodden ballplayers might have been a superlative public relations move. It would be a stretch of logic to believe that Haywood's "one big strike by one big union" might have begun here, but the threat of such could have done the desperate ballplayers little harm.

This intervention couldn't have hurt "Big Bill" much either. One would suspect that baseball might well have been a welcome distraction to many of those laboring seemingly endless hours in a mine or a plant. Such an individual might well sympathize with the distressing events that the Black Sox were experiencing. Why not, "If they want war, let it begin here"?

---

[228]    http://www.crf.usa.org./broa/bria17_2.htm page 1. Accessed 25 June, 2005.

In spite of all of the vigor, "Big Bill" Haywood was able to bring to the labor movement his "days were numbered." It is quite possible that by the early twenties the International Workers of the World could not muster the support needed to back the type of campaign that the Black Sox would need.

While the communist view of baseball was not overly sympathetic, "the doctrine" seemed to fall in line with the rest of the beliefs against those who toiled for profit. As always, the owners of the industry were the primary target. Michael Gold seemed to summarize those beliefs in a chapter titled, "Baseball is a Racket" in his book *CHANGE THE WORLD!* "Workers love baseball. But baseball, in its own way, is used as 'opium of the people.' The 'bosses' are cashing in on the 'heroes' and cashing in on the frustrated love of the people."[229] At this point in history it would seem that it would not only be the duty of a communist leader to "liberate" the poor, mistreated baseball laborers, but a great public relations move as well.

Before Haywood exited the American labor scene we certainly would have asked: "Hey Bill, if you believe as you say you do, you can't just abandon our guys to the 'wolves of industry.' Could any of your contacts in the CPUSA have enough labor skills that could do us any good?" Perhaps he and his party would accept such a challenge. "The boys" were not communists. Our eight were merely poor American labor. Still, with our situation being so desperate, we would take our help where we could find it. The CPUSA was not a deplorable organization in the 1920s and often they would stand up for the worker who was, virtually standing alone.

Within a decade Haywood would die in Russia where he had fled to avoid imprisonment. By then the IWW was little more than a fading memory. Perhaps turning the tide for these

---

[229] Michael Gold, *CHANGE THE WORLD.* (International Publications. New York. 1936) 101.

Chicago baseball players could have been a lasting tribute to the International Workers of the World. This cause certainly would have been a worthy venting of otherwise unusable energy. Although an "unqualified victory" might not have been achieved, perhaps as with the "Lawrence Strike" the gain would have made the sacrifice worthwhile. While it was probably too late for the Wobblies to change the course of history, one last "big hurrah" certainly should have been worth the effort.

I am sure that forces larger than baseball in the Nation's economic leadership could have been convinced to take an interest. Some of Judge Landis' old friends in Washington might have advised that baseball cut its losses. Labor unrest within "the National Past time" could well have been more than Congress was prepared to put up with after all the country had recently been through. The watch words may well have been to "compromise and settle."

I believe the IWW would have helped. In the words of Melvyn Dubofsky and Foster Rhea Dulles: "…this revolutionary movement spectacularly centered attention on the desperate needs of vast numbers of unskilled workers…"[230] The Black Sox were definitely desperate, this certainly would have been an avenue worth exploring

As the process went along, so would the media blitz. The Chicago Tribune which had headlined of the ballplayers' confessions would later read, "What Confessions?" Thank you Mr. Rothstein! Comiskey's offer of a $100,000 reward would have been heavily played. The reward was never paid. Perhaps further headlines. "Charlie, do you want the truth"? A few days later another one "Comiskey put your money where you mouth is!"

If the Tribune wouldn't print such headlines, many other papers in the country certainly would. "Thus, labor newspapers

---

[230]   Melvin Dubofsky and Foster Rhea Dulles, <u>LABOR IN AMERICA</u> (Wheeling, Illinois, Harlan Davidson, 1999) 208.

and other publications became popular to bolster the fight for the rights of workers across the nation."[231] We are sure that there were cases in which the American worker would trust these tabloids better than the large, corporate owned journals. We would have contacted the editors of these tabloids often enough to become on a "first name basis" with them. "Have your members contacted their congresspersons regarding the Blacksox? Written any good 'Joe Jackson, Buck Weaver articles 'lately? Need to sell any advertising space?" If baseball was trying to forget our players, we would assure that labor would not!

To a large extent eight men were portrayed as villains so that others, also guilty, could escape. Ultimately, the public may have risen to the defense of the players when they understood the environment in which the 1919 World Series was played.

As much as a love for baseball, Charles Comiskey was motivated by money. The 1921 season would have been one critical to the defense of the Black Sox. That year the Cubs actually played better than the remaining Chicago White Sox. Neither team was very good. The "North Siders" were 64-89 in the National League. The remainder of Comiskey's team was even worse, going 62-92 in the American League. We would organize visits to Cub Park centered around baseball's three big pre media paydays. "Show your support for the aggrieved ballplayers skip the Sox and come north" on Memorial Day, the 4th of July and Labor Day. "Hey Charlie, can you hear those Cub turnstiles rolling? Wanna Talk?" A mutually agreeable settlement would have, no doubt, been much easier before both sides in the confrontation spent the rest of their lives throwing mud at each other.

We would have challenged the election of Kenesaw Mountain Landis as Commissioner of all of baseball. We would argue that the presumption of authority by the American and National Leagues upon the rest of baseball was arbitrary and presumptuous. We

---

[231] Godfried. <u>WCFL; CHICAGO'S VOICE OF LABOR 1926-78.</u> 10.

would turn the matter over to our attorneys. It is expected that by the time this matter was resolved in court, all of Judge Landis' ninety plus years on this earth would have expired and that he would no longer be in a position to deprive the Black Sox of their opportunity to make a living.

Should the affront to Landis' authority fail it would only be the beginning of our appeals. As the lifetime suspensions were handed out to the ballplayers, Judge Landis would be accused of an "ex post facto" ruling that was depriving the eight men of the opportunity to earn a living. It would be necessary to put forth the question of Judge Landis' judicial record prior to baseball. Was Landis a compassionate ruler or a reincarnation of Judge Roy Beam? The "Standard Oil Decision" and its later modification would have been presented as an example of Judge Landis' propensity for excess and showmanship.

If necessary we would insert Jimmy O'Connell and Cozey Dolan into the mix. These two players were suspended by the Commissioner for allegedly offering Phillies' shortstop Heinie Sand five hundred dollars to "throw" a game on September 23, 1924. When questioned, O'Connell indicated that he had made the offer "in jest." Poor Jimmy, a really bad time to make a joke. Dolan replied that "I just don't remember" when confronted with the allegations.[232] End of "due process." Landis suspended two more players for life. Was the Commissioner "high handed"? The times, they are a changin'.

In the event that "KML" and the club owners could not yet "smell their goose cooking" we have an additional alternative. Sports owners loathe competition for labor services. In the second half of the Twentieth Century both the American Football League and the American Basketball Association brought existing leagues to compromise by driving salaries up. We would have

---

[232]  http://www.1919blackson.xom/banished.htm. 2. Accessed 22 June, 2004.

approached those owners of Federal League teams who had been "cut out" of the settlement with the American and National Leagues. There were, no doubt, still usable ballparks in the old Federal League Cities. Kansas City, Baltimore, Buffalo and Indianapolis had shown an interest in "big league enterprise." A revival in the other four cities would have been even more interesting. Brooklyn, St. Louis, Pittsburgh and, yes, Chicago. Nothing drives up the cost of labor services as much as competition. Rising labor cost and the prospect of another "Reserve Clause" battle in court might well have been enough to turn "The Old Roman's" stomach. It could also have caused him to talk "turkey" with my clients. One big name Black Sox player to each franchise could have made money for new baseball ownership. Our guess is that Comiskey would choose not to do battle with the likes of the Chicago Whales again. "Have ballplayers, will travel." There was additional talent to be employed that the baseball fan might recognize. Mordecai "Three Finger" Brown, Joe Tinker, George Mullin and Al Bridwell were available.[233] While each of these players might not have been employed on the diamond, some were well past their prime, the public relations value would have been enormous. This offer may have been commence rate with "running a bluff," but with Federal League memories so fresh in the owners' minds, they may have ordered the Commissioner to make a deal. If the leader had used his "absolute power" the worse that might have been accomplished was to drive a wedge between "the general and his troops." The odds would then become better than "eight against the world."

233  http://www.historicbaseball.com/federalleague.html. 2. Accessed 27 June, 2005.

# CHAPTER EIGHTEEN

If all of our efforts at "justice" had failed, the Black Sox would still be no worse than they were in November of 1920. That having been said, let us see how the lives of the Black Sox played out after their baseball careers. To a large extent, these men lived lives very similar to the millions of middle age men in the United States during the first half of the Twentieth Century who had never been touched by an occupation in professional sports.

The Black Sox general outlasted their adversaries. That "the establishment" died off first is more a testimony to the difference in age between the participants than a declaration of "truth and justice." Charles A. Comiskey Sr. ceased his duties as owner/operator of the Chicago White Sox on October 26, 1931. Only death could have caused such a division.

There is a widely reported legend that the president of the American League visited with Comiskey shortly before the death of the White Sox owner. The story says that Johnson offered his hand as a gesture of friendship and forgiveness. The legend says that the effort of handshake was refused. Those who knew have long departed, who knows? Ban Johnson passed on February 28, 1931 after a long illness.[234]

The loyal Kid Gleason led the White Sox through the darkest period of their history. He was the manager through the 1923 season. After taking a couple of seasons away from the game Gleason hired on as a coach for Connie Mack's Philadelphia A's. Philadelphia would earn the Kid trips back to the World Series in 1930 and 1931. Now nicknamed "Pop" Gleason coached while

[234]   http://www.baseballlibrary.com/baseballlibrary/ballplayers/J/Johnson_Ban.stm. 1. Accessed 1 October, 2005.

seriously ill in 1932. A "baseball man" to the end, Gleason died of a heart ailment January 2, 1933 in Philadelphia.[235]

Kennesaw Mountain Landis moved on to a higher court on November 25, 1944 in Chicago. The cause of death was a heart attack. It is ironic that this would be the cause of demise of someone with "such a strong heart." The Judge was seventy eight years old. Time reeks vengeance upon all humankind. As Landis led baseball through the traumatic "post scandal" period, he was granted power that no commissioner has enjoyed since. Landis was a cure that was, apparently, better than the disease.

Eddie Collins was long expected to succeed Connie Mack as manager of the Philadelphia Athletics. It's a good thing Cocky didn't wait. Mack managed the club until 1950 when he was eighty eight years old. Some might have contributed this longevity to "ego." "The Tall Tactician," did in fact own and operate the franchise in addition to his on the field duties. To those who doubt Mack's ability it should be pointed out that he led "his" team to nine American League pennants and five World Championships. Mack may have had some justification if he felt that there was no candidate more qualified to manage the Philadelphia Athletics than the owner himself.

Eddie switched to the Boston Red Sox when former prep school classmate Tom Yawkey inherited the team. During his tenure in Boston E. Collins was responsible for signing Hall of Famers Bobby Doerr and Ted Williams to the club. Eddie survived Connie Mack by only one year.

Ray Schalk was inducted into the Hall of Fame in 1955. Some time after his retirement Schalk selected his "all teammate team." Kid Gleason was, of course, the manager. Buck Crouse was the catcher (Cracker, of course, couldn't name himself.) It is presumed if Crouse were naming a similar team Schalk would

235 "William "Kid" Gleason." http://www.dvrbs.com/CamdenSports-KidG-leason.htm. 2. Accessed 4 October, 2005.

be behind the plate. "Cocky" and Red Faber were on the squad. Happy and Eddie Cicotte were also there. Joe Jackson was not selected. People disagree. It would seem that Schalk did a magnificent job of being fair to all of his teammates. We would have expected no less![236] Cracker died May 19, 1970 in Chicago.

Joe Jackson became a phenomenally successful businessman back "home" in his native South Carolina. Joe completed his life less bitter than one would have expected from the time he spent "in the north."

Bucky knew that he had been cheated. It was reported in the December 14, 1920 issue of "Collyer's Eye" that Comiskey had promised Weaver that he would be reinstated with the White Sox if acquitted in court.[237] It never happened. Bucky was the saddest of all of these players. He was the only suspended Chicago player to remain in that metropolitan area. He continued to earn a living doing "odd jobs" in the Chicago area. He helped repaint the Cook County Courthouse, home of the Chicago Grand Jury (nice?) Weaver worked for a time as a pharmacist with his brother in law. He campaigned for his reinstatement until his death in 1956.

Perhaps the best judgment of Weaver as a baseball player can be gained by comments from his peers given shortly after his death. *The Sporting News,* then considered "the Baseball Bible" by many experts gave comment on Weaver's passing from Red Faber and Ray Schalk. The thoughts should be considered particularly revealing from two of the men who played the 1919 World Series "on the square." The tabloid notes that each man was "emotionally shaken" by the passing of the third baseman.

"Each called Weaver 'the greatest third baseman that I ever saw.' Neither, however, would discuss Weaver's alleged connection with the 1919 Black Sox.

---

[236]  http://www.thebaseballpage.com/past/pp/schalkray/. 1. Accessed 14 October, 2005.
[237]  http://www.clearbuck.com/bio.htm. 2. Accessed 17 July, 2005.

'The incident caused Weaver the torture of hell,' said Schalk. 'Anything that I can say about Weaver is to boost him…'

'I played baseball with Weaver and I played cards with him' said Faber. 'And I found him to be as honest as could be. No one can ever be certain about 1919, I guess. Weaver was a wonderful competitor. A fellow who played baseball because he loved it.' [238] Such comments are on Hall of Fame plaques, but not for Bucky. It's a shame!

In spite of all his suffering "Eddie lost the farm." Cicotte lived, mostly, under assumed names. While game warden, security guard and snow sweeper are noble occupations, one of the greatest right handed pitchers in baseball deserved better from the game. "Knuckles" died May 5, 1969, back home in Detroit. His headstone bears his real name. At peace- at last.

Happy, too, got tired of arguing and eventually just gave up. He was seventy three when laid to rest in Milwaukee. Lefty, he of excellent control and the great fastball ran a pool hall and just barely got by in Chicago until moving to California where he died in Laguna Beach in 1959.

After, and perhaps because of, the ruling by Judge Landis, the Swede still wanted something from baseball. Felsch and Risberg may have been looking for justice, perhaps only vengeance. No matter what the motive the two sued the White Sox for over four hundred thousand dollars for back pay and damage to their reputations.[239] They were less successful than Jackson in the legal arena and the suit was dismissed.

Risberg was not done battling with baseball yet. In 1927 Judge Landis held hearings to investigate charges brought by the former shortstop that several Detroit players had thrown games to help the Chicago White Sox win the pennant. The

[238] "Buck Weaver Dead at 64; Denied 'Black Sox' Charge." The Sporting News. February 8, 1956. 30.
[239] http://www.baseballlibrary.com/baseballlibrary/ballplayers/R/Risberg_Swede.stm. Accessed 28 August 2005.

only witnesses coming forth for Risberg were Gandil and Felsch. Landis dismissed the case. It was evident that baseball gave no credibility to these men. The world was all too familiar with "sour grapes." Were these men acting of bitterness to the team that had achieved the World Championship that they had given away? Could it have been also that Landis would not permit another scandal so soon after such an embarrassment had nearly ruined the industry that paid him a handsome salary? Each individual must form judgments in this matter based solely upon their own beliefs in those telling the story. It was clear that Chick, Hap and the Swede were not leaving baseball on amicable terms.

Lefty moved to California. He and his wife Lyria first settled in the San Fernando Valley. Later they operated a nursery business in Laguna Beach until the time of Claude's death, November 4, 1959 following an extended illness. Lefty was sixty six.[240]

After many years of dairy farming in Minnesota, on October 13, 1975 Charles "Swede" Risberg the last survivor of our eight conspirators died in Red Bluff, California. It was his eighty first birthday. *THE SPORTING NEWS* eulogized Risberg "Risberg was only twenty five when he jumped into the fix stew. He was a rangy good fielding shortstop but a modest hitter."[241] This passing of the final member of the eight Black Sox would seem to have ended all earthly consequences of the "Black Sox Scandal"- save one! A discussion of the 1919 Chicago Black Sox must include the question: Why are none of these men in baseball's Hall of Fame. Judge Landis has been enshrined in Cooperstown. Charles Comiskey, Red Faber and Eddie Collins all have "space." None of our eight players have been inducted. The "lifetime suspensions" had apparently become "death time bans" as well. Actually, only two could have ever been considered. Eddie Cicotte and Joe Jackson were the

---

[240]   "Obituaries." *THE SPORTING NEWS.* November 18, 1959 18.
[241]   "Obituaries." *THE SPORTING NEWS.* November 1, 1975. 26.

only of our players who played the ten years in the major leagues to meet minimum eligibility standards. For seventy years voters overlooked these two, although all of their activities on the field, save October 1919 would have warranted inclusion.

# CHAPTER NINETEEN

By 1989 another "scandal" in baseball required action. In response to the "Peter Rose situation" Faye Vincent acting on behalf of Commissioner A. Bartlett Giomotti convinced the Hall of Fame executive board to create a "Permanently ineligible for Induction" list. This action precluded anyone who was ineligible to participate in the major leagues at the conclusion of there career from being considered for "The Hall." In addition to Rose, Cicotte and Jackson several other former participants "went down with the ship"at this point. While it is possible to apply for reinstatement, no one has successfully made such and effort on behalf of Joe and Eddie to date. Our players were "done in"by Commissioners twice- eighty years apart.

It is our guess that labor actions similar to those we have proposed may have caused the leaders of professional baseball to modify the suspensions to something less than "lifetime." Knowing the dispositions of Comiskey and Landis, there might have been no change in the discipline at all. At the very least the Twenty First Century observer could be confident that justice was done for eight simple men. Certainly this author would feel much better about this portion of baseball history. Much more important, I believe a true process of justice is all that "The Black Sox" would have ever asked for.

Alfred, Lord Tennyson wrote that: "'Tis Better to have loved and lost, than never loved at all."[242] I have spent considerable time reflecting upon the Black Sox and the 1919 World Series. I believe that baseball was better after the scandal subsided and the operation was forced to clean its own house. Without the Black Sox and the actions of

Commissioner Landis the game may have evolved as

---

[242] http://www.trivia-library.com/b/origins-of-sayings-tis-better-tso-have-loved-and-lost.html accessed 25 June, 2005

professional wrestling and never become the billion dollar industry that it is today. To this extent, baseball was saved.

Would these Chicago players have been better to never have
loved the game at all? Baseball brought Eddie Cicotte, Lefty
Williams, Chick Gandil, the Swede Risberg, Freddie McMullin,
Buck Weaver, Happy Felsch and Joe Jackson fame. Later it also
brought them infamy. The lifetime ban they were administered
for their actions has been, since the 1970s a "death time" sentence as well.

In at least one way the Black Sox would have been better
served had they been convicted by the Grand Jury. Such action
would have brought an appeal process through the court system.
A request for clemency would have been filed with the gover-
nor of Illinois. An injunction could have been filed preventing
baseball from depriving the players of the right to make a living.
In short, there are avenues for guilty men. For over eighty years
those who believe that these men were mistreated have been left
with the question: "How do you appeal a 'not guilty' sentence?"

I believe that this work has made it evident that the author
is: "A Black Sox fan." If you want to be sad, take a few minutes
someday and read "This Is the Truth."[243] This article for *SPORT
MAGAZINE* was written by Furman Bisher in October, 1949.
The interviews took place on Joe's front porch in South Carolina.
It is almost certain that the memory was not of perfect fact. It
could not be expected to be after thirty years had passed. The
interview was important in a different way. Bisher portrayed
Jackson as a simple, contented man. Life, with the possible exception of major league baseball had been good to him. He spoke
with kindness of everyone he mentioned within the sport. A hero
within his state. Too good a man to have died with the blemish
still attached to his name. They all were!

---

[243] Joseph Jefferson Jackson and Furman Bisher. "This is the Truth." www.
law.umke.edu.faculty/projects/ftrials/blacksox/jacksonstory.html. Accessed 8 July, 2005.

It is difficult to nearly impossible to "like" such diverse personalities as Joe Jackson, Eddie Cicotte, Charlie Comiskey and Kennesaw Mountain Landis. Still, it is as though each one of the men involved in "The Scandal" were standing at the "you are here" sign in a shopping mall. Each chose to enter a different department store. Simultaneously, all were right and each was wrong.

Victor Luhrs author of the work: THE GREAT BASEBALL MYSTERY: THE 1919 WORLD SERIES was used as a source for this material. Luhrs appears to have been, as I, a "Black Sox fan." The last chapter of his book is titled: "Some Conclusions (Probably Erroneous.) Any "conclusions" or opinions of events so long past are likely to contain flaws. Victor presents an emotional argument that this World Series was not "thrown." The comparative statistics he presents between the "Black" and "White" Sox are interesting and enjoyable. I wish I could believe! Unfortunately, the Eliot Asinof material seems to lead to a more valid conclusion. It is not always how badly the game is played that determines the outcome. Sometimes the pivotal factor is "when the game is played badly." This evaluation would seem to leave little room to contend that my unfortunate friends were "not guilty." Still, one must pause to think that after all of these years the "punishment" has far exceeded the"crime." The feeling that linger should, perhaps, be only of peace and understanding for all who endured the events consequential to the 1919 World Series.

As all humans, each succeeded as well as failed in their efforts. Forgiveness for all is long overdue. I have but one wish left for my friends, the Black Sox and those who administered punishment to them. Let us finally declare "peace." Someday a statement should be issued that justice has long ago been served. I believe that it has! The 1919 Chicago American League team contained no men who betrayed sensitive military secrets of their country none committed murder. This group should once again be considered one team. Has baseball finally grown big enough to say to all "you are forgiven"? I believe it has!

# BIBLIOGRAPHY

Primary Sources

Asinof, Eliot: <u>EIGHT MEN OUT</u> New York: Henry Holt and Company. 1963.

Bisher, Furman and Jackson, Joseph Jefferson. "This is the Truth." http://www.lse.umke.edu/faculty/projects/blacksox/jackson-story.htm

Miller, Benjamin E. MD. <u>THE COMPLETE MEDICAL GUIDE.</u> "Diseases of the Kidney." Simon and Schuster. 1978.

"Rising Salaries of Baseball and the Reserve Clause." http:www.wow essays.com.


Secondary Sources

"An Arnold Rothstein Chronology." David Pietrusza. http://www.davidpietrusza.com/Rothstein-Chronology.html.

"Arnold Rothstein (1882-1928) Criminal Mastermind." http://www.carpenoctem.tv/mafia/rothstein.html.

"Ban Johnson." http://www.baseballlibrary.com/baseballlibrary/ballplayers/J/Johnson_Ban.stm.

Barrett. James R. <u>WORK AND COMMUNITY IN THE JUNGLE.</u> Urbana, Illinois and Chicago. University of Illinois Press. 1987

"Banished from Baseball." http//www.1919blacksox.comhtml.

"Bill Rariden." http://www.baseballlibrary.com/baseballlibrary/ballplayers/R/Rariden_Bill.stm.

"Biographical Directory of the United States Congress 1776-Present." http://bioguide.congress.gov/biosearch/biosearch1.asp.

"Bombers Honor Jackson." http://nl.newsbreak.com/nl-search/we/Arcive?s_sote=greemvo;;epm;oml&f_site=greenvilleo_.

Brody, David. LABOR IN CRISIS: THE STEEL STRIKE OF 1919. Urbana, Illinois and Chicago. University of Illinois Press. 1987.

Brody, David. STEELWORKERS IN AMERICA: THE NONUNION ERA. Urbana, Illinois and Chicago. University of Illinois Press. 1998.

"The Chicago Blacksox."http/www.chs.org/history/blacksox/blk4. ht

"Charlie Comiskey." http//www.baseball library.com/baseball library/ballplayers/C/Comiskey_Charlie.stm

"Crosley Field, a.k.a. Redland Field." http:www.baseball-statistics.com/ballparks/Cin/Crosley.htm.

Dubofsky, Melvyn and Dulles, Foster Rhea. LABOR IN AMERICA Wheeling, Illinois. 1999.

D. A. Eastren, Theodore Morse and Arthur Sullivan. "Hail, Hail, the Gangs All Here."

"Dolf Luque." http://www/baseballlibrary.com/baseballlibrary/ballplayers/L/Luque_Dolf.stm.

"Dutch Ruether." http://www.baseballlibrary.com/baseballlibrary/ballplayers/R/Ruether_Dutch_stm.

"Edd Rousch." http://www/baseballlibrary.com/baselllirary/ballplayers/R/Rousch_Edd.stm.

"Eddie Collins." http://www/baseballlibrary.com/baseballlibrary/ballplayers/C/Collins_Eddie.stm.

"Eddie Collins." http://www.baseballreference.com/collied01.shtml.

"Eddie Collins Jr." http://www.baseballreference.com/collied02.stml.

"Federal League." Http/www.historic baseball.com/federalleague.html

Godfried, Nathan. WCFL CHICAGO'S VOICE OF LABOR 1926-78. University of Illinois Press. Urbana, Illinois and Chicago. 1987.

Gold, Michael. CHANGE THE WORLD!. International Publishers. New York. 1936,

"Greasy Neale." http://www.baseballlibrary.com/baseballlibrary/ballplayers/N/Neale_Greasy.stm.

Guttersioh, H. K. "Follett, 'Black Sox' Niece, Dies at 89." http://nl.newsbreat.com/nl-search/we/Archives?p_action+doc&p_docid+OFE5052B60ACC_. Accessed 10 July 2005.

"Hal Chase." http://www.baseballlibrary.com/baseballlibrary/ballplayers/C/Chase_Hal.stm.

"Hal Chase Statistics." http://www.baseball-reference.cin/c/chaseha01.shtml.

"Heinie Groh." http//www.baseballlibrary.com/baseball library/ballplayers/Groh_Heinie.stm.

"Hod Eller." http//www.baseballlibrary.com./baseball library/ballplayers/Eller_Hod.stm.

"Horse Shoe Nail." http:// www.callings.freserve.co

"Theatrical Stage Employees Local One." http://www.iatselocal-one.org/about/history.html.
"IATSE Local #2 Chicago History." http://iatselocal2.com/history/history.shtml.

"IATSE Local #2: Chicago About." http://iatselocal2.com/about/about.shtml.

"Ivy Wingo." http://www.baseballlibrary.com/baseballlibrary/ballplayers/W/Wingo_Ivy.stm

"Jake Daubert." http// www.baseballlibrary.com/baseball library/ballplayers/D/Daubert_Jake.stm.

"Jimmy Ring." http// www.baseball library.com/ baseball library/ballplayers/R/Ring_ Jimmy.stm.. Accessed 25 September 2005.

"Jimmy Smith." http://www.baseballlibrary.com/baseballlibrary/ballplayers/S/Smith_Jimmy.stm

"John Greenleaf Whittier (1807-1892). http://www.bartleby.com/100/439.5html.

LABOR STUDIES IN THE WORKING CLASS HISTORY OF AMERICA: VOLUME 2; NUMBER 1; SPRING 2005. Labor and Working Class History Association. 2005.

"La Follette, Robert M(arion)." http://searcheb.com/elections/micro/333/3html. Accessed 16 July, 2005.

"Larry Kopf." http://www.baseballlibrary.com/baseballlibrary/K/Kopf_Larry.stm

Linder, Douglas. "The Black Sox Trial: An Account." http://www.law.umke.edu/faculty/projects/trials/blacksox/blacksoxaccount.c

Luhrs, Victor. THE GREAT BASEBALL MYSTERY; THE 1919 WORLD SERIES. South Brunswick, New Jersey. A. S. Barnes and Company. 1966,

"MLB Player Profile for Shano Collins." http://www.sportspool.com/baseball/players/C/collish01.php.

"Maurice Rath." www.baseballlibrary.com/baseballlibrary/ballplayers/R/Rath_Maurice.stm.

"Mary Harris (Mother) Jones." http://digitallibrary.upenn.edu/women/Jones/Mother/Jones.html.

"1919 World Series Game 1." http://www.blackbetsy.com/19game1.htm.

"1919 World Series Game 2." http://www.blackbetsy.com/19game2. htm.

"1919 World Series Game 3." http://www.blackbetsy.com/19game3. htm.

"1919 World Series Game 4." http://www.blackbetsy.com/19game4. htm.

"1919 World Series Game 5." http://www.blackbetsy.com/19game5. htm.

"1919 World Series Game 6." http://www.blackbetsy.com/19game6. htm.

"1919 World Series Game 7." http://www.blackbetsy.com/19game7. htm.

"1919 World Series Game 8." http://www.blackbetsy.com/19game8. htm.

www.paperofrecord.com.

"Pat Duncan." http://www.baseballlibrary.com/baseballlibrary/ ballplayers/D/Duncan.stm

Peter Palmer and Gary Gilette. THE ENCYCLOPEDIA OF BASEBALL. New York. Barnes and Nobel. 2004.

David Pietrusza. "Rothstein." http://www.davidpietrusza.com/ Rothstein.html

"Origins of Sayings." http/www.trivia- library.com.

"Outlaw Baseball Players in the Copper League 1925-1927." http://wwwbevillsadvocate.org/histwebCHAPTER4.html.

"Pat Moran." http://www.baseballlibrary.com/ballplayers/M/Moran-Pat.stm

"Ray Fisher." http://www.baseballlibrary.com/baseballlibrary/ballplayers/F/Fisher_Ray.stm.

"Ray Schalk." http://www.baseballhalloffame.org/hofers_and_honoreees/hofer_bios/schalk_ray.htm.

"Ray Schalk." http://en.wikipedia.org/wiki/Ray_Schal

"Ray Schalk." http://www.thebaseballpage.com?past/pp/schalkray/.

"Ray Schalk." http://www.baseball-reference.com/managers/schalra.shtml.

"Ray Schalk Baseball Stats by Baseball Almanac." http://www.baseball-almanac.com/players/player.php?p=schalra01.

"Ray Schalk." http://www.baseball-reference.com/s/schalra01.stml.

"Raymond William Schalk: 'Cracker.' http://www.baseball-statistics.com/HOF/Schalk.html.

"Shano Collins." http://www.baseballlibrary.com/baseballlibrary/ballplayers/C/Collins_Shano.stm.

"Sherry Magee." http://www.baseballlibrary.com/baseballlibrary/ballplayers/M/Magee_Sherry.stm.

"Slim Salee." http://www.baseballlibrary.com/baseballlibrary/ballplayers/S/Salee_Slim.stm

"Buck Weaver Dead at 64; Denied 'Black Sox' Charge." *THE SPORTING NEWS.* St. Louis. February 8. 1956. 30.

"NL Spins Back Clock With Festival at Birthplace." *YHE SPORTING NEWS.* St. Louis. February 14. 1951. Page 6.

"Red Faber." http://www.baseballlibrary.com/baseballlibrary/ballplayers/F/Faber_Red/stm

Robert Smith. <u>PIONEERS OF BASEBALL.</u> Boston and Toronto. Robert Smith. 1976.

"The Sporting News." http://www.paperofrecord.com./Default.asp.

"The 10 Most Famous Sherlock Holmes Story Quotations." http://members.aol.com/_lit_a/shbest/quote/Tqhm.htm.

"U.S. Cellular Field (a. k .a) Comiskey Park." http://www.base-ball-statistics.com/ballparks/ChiWS/Comiskey.htm.

"What's In A Name?" http://www.crimelibrary.com/gangster_outlaws/mob_bosses/Rothstein/index_1.html

"William J. 'Kid' Gleason." http://www.dvrbs.com/CamdenSports-KidGleason.htm.

"William J. "Kid" Gleason." http://www.baseballlegends.com./ballplayers/G/Gleason_Kid/stm.

"The Wobblies, Unions, Workers Strike, Lubbites, Genaral Ludd in Industrial Relations." http://www.crf-usa.org/bria/bral_2. html.

J.G. Taylor Spink: <u>JUDGE LANDIS AND TWENTY-FIVE YEARS OF BASEBALL.</u> New York. Thomas Y. Crowell and Company. 1947.